STARTING OVER

"You know," Sally said, "this is so incredibly different from, well—" She broke off, searching for the right words. She faced Dana with a look of wonder on her face. "I've never lived in such a nice place before."

"Listen, forget about it, OK?" Dana said. "You live with us now, so you don't have to think about your old life. You can just pretend it never happened, right?" She paused, looking carefully at her cousin's face. "Right?" she insisted.

A look of surprise crossed Sally's features. "Oh, sure, I'll just try to forget about it."

Behind Sally's back, Dana scowled. She was concentrating on creating a new Sally, but Sally insisted on bringing up the past. "Listen, I really think you should think about the future," said Dana.

She looked intently into Sally's face, searching for signs of agreement. After a moment, Sally dropped her eyes to her lap and nodded. "If you say so, Dana."

Bantam Books in the Sweet Valley High Series
Ask your bookseller for the books you have missed

SWEET VALLEY HIGH

STARTING OVER

Written by
Kate William

Created by
FRANCINE PASCAL

BANTAM BOOKS
TORONTO · NEW YORK · LONDON · SYDNEY · AUCKLAND

RL, IL age 12 and up

STARTING OVER
A Bantam Book / January 1987
6 printings through February 1988

Sweet Valley High is a trademark of Francine Pascal.

Conceived by Francine Pascal.

Produced by Cloverdale Press, Inc.,
133 Fifth Ave., New York, N.Y. 10003.

Cover art by James Mathewuse.

ISBN 0-553-27491-0

Published simultaneously in the United States and Canada

Bantam Books are published by Bantam Books, a division of Bantam Doubleday Dell Publishing Group, Inc. Its trademark, consisting of the words ''Bantam Books'' and the portrayal of a rooster, is Registered in U.S. Patent and Trademark Office and in other countries. Marca Registrada. Bantam Books, 666 Fifth Avenue, New York, New York 10103.

PRINTED IN THE UNITED STATES OF AMERICA

O   15   14   13   12   11   10   9   8   7

STARTING OVER

One

"Dana, I said let's take it from the beginning again, OK? We're doing 'Meltdown.' "

Dana Larson was startled out of her thoughts. Guy Chesney, the keyboard player for The Droids, Sweet Valley High's most popular band, was looking at her impatiently, waiting for her to snap out of her reverie.

"Hey, sorry, you guys," The Droids' leader singer said with a self-mocking smile. "I guess I was in outer space for a minute there," she added, looking around at the familiar faces in the basement of lead guitarist Max Dellon's house.

"Yeah, well, come on back to Sweet Valley, OK? That's where we're practicing—at least for *this* Friday afternoon."

Dana smiled weakly. She *had* been far away. She was thinking about her cousin, Sally Lar-

1

son, who was arriving that night to live with Dana's family for a while. Dana hadn't seen Sally since they were very small. Back then, Dana had envied Sally. After all, she was a year older than Dana and it seemed to make a big difference. But she didn't envy Sally any more.

After Sally's father had left home thirteen years before, Sally's mother had remarried and given her up to a foster home. When that hadn't worked out, she was sent to another.

For years, Dana's cousin had been bouncing from one home to another. She'd even had to drop back a year in school, because she'd missed so much. Who knew how all that shuffling around had changed Sally, Dana mused.

As she forced her attention on rehearsal, Dana was still preoccupied. She wasn't sure how to break the news to her friends in the band. They were just about the most important people in her life: The Droids spent so much time together, practicing for and playing gigs, that they were like a second family to Dana. So she wanted to tell them about Sally.

The only problem was that Sally's situation was embarrassing. A father who was a bum, no real home, a year behind in school. Sure, it wasn't Sally's fault, but . . .

They ran through "Meltdown," but Dana couldn't really concentrate. When they had finished, Dana said, "Listen, everybody, I've got an announcement to make." She ran her fingers through her cropped hair. It felt strange to be nervous about talking to the other Droids.

Dana looked at her fellow band members. Emily Mayer was sitting behind the drums, beating a tempo softly on the rim of a snare. In the corner, Max Dellon was leaning against his amplifier with his guitar hanging in front of him, and Dan Scott, the bass guitarist, was sitting next to him on another amplifier. Behind the keyboard, Guy was picking out a quiet melody.

"So, what's the big announcement, Dana?" Guy asked finally, looking up from the keys.

She laughed. "I don't know why I'm making such a big deal about it. I just wanted to tell you that my cousin Sally is coming to stay with my family for a while. She'll be going to school here."

Quiet, dark-haired Emily smiled. "Hey, that's great, Dana! Think she'll want to watch us practice?"

Shrugging her shoulders, Dana looked from one band member to another. "I hadn't thought about it, but if you guys don't mind, maybe it would be a good way to get her involved, get right into the action." She was greeted by nods and smiles.

"Sure, no problem," Max said. "It never hurts to have a fresh ear listen to us, keep us from getting lazy, you know? Does she play?"

"Well, actually, I don't know." Dana laughed, a little embarrassed. "I don't really know too much about her, to tell the truth. I haven't even seen her since we were little."

Emily spoke again. "How old is she?"

That was one direct question Dana didn't want to answer. "She's a junior," she said, after a moment's hesitation.

Dan, who was sorting through some sheet music, looked up. "So when do we get to check her out?"

"Well, she's coming tonight, so Monday, I guess. I'll bring her to practice, OK?"

The Droids nodded. "Sure, no problem," Guy repeated. "Let's call it quits for today, anyway. I told Lynne I'd take her to dinner."

Dana breathed a sigh of relief. She didn't know why she was so nervous. She told herself firmly that Sally would probably turn out to be a great kid and she'd really like her.

The band busied itself, putting away instruments and picking up school books. But Dana was still distracted. She couldn't stop thinking about Sally, wondering what she would be like and how they would get along. What would she look like? Would Sally like old movies as much as Dana did? What kind of music did she listen to?

She became more excited when she got home. In a few hours, another person would be living there. She went into the kitchen for a snack and found her brother, Jeremy, pouring himself a bowl of cereal. Jeremy was a year older than Dana and was a senior at Sweet Valley High.

"I can't believe Sally will be here tonight," Dana said, getting a bowl and spoon and pouring some cereal for herself. She hopped up on a stool and reached for the new issue of *Rolling Stone*. Anticipation was making it hard for her to concentrate, and she barely glanced at the articles in her favorite magazine. Finally, she gave up trying to read. "I just can't believe it," she said, taking a spoonful of cereal.

Jeremy grunted. "Yeah. Me neither."

"Hey, come on, Jer." She looked into her brother's dark brown eyes, which were clouded with annoyance. "Aren't you kind of excited about it? Don't you wonder what kind of person she is? Whether you'll like her?"

"No," he said.

"Jeremy, I mean, it'll be like having another sister."

"Ha!" He snorted, bringing the spoon to his mouth. "That's all I need is another sister," he mumbled through a mouthful of cornflakes.

"Sorry! I didn't know it was such a burden to live with me."

"Well, come on," he complained. "I mean, out of the blue comes this cousin we haven't seen in years, and I get talked out of my room and have to move into the attic. The attic!"

Dana made a sour face at her brother. "Oh, Jerry, lighten up. You know the attic is like a

5

whole separate apartment. It'll be much better living up there."

"Yeah, well, I wish Mom and Dad would lay off about this whole welcome wagon stuff," Jeremy stormed on. "You'd think she was some kind of princess or a cripple or something. 'Be nice, kids,' " he mimicked in a high voice. " 'Try to be sensitive and thoughtful. Sally's had a hard time.' God, I'm already sick of her!"

Dana stared at him in surprise. "What's gotten into you?"

He placed his bowl in the sink with a clatter. "Nothing. There are just too many people in my life already, OK? I'm going over to Mark's." Facing his sister, he added defiantly, "And I may stay for dinner."

"All right. Jeez, chill out, Jerry. You don't have to get so wired up about it." Dana raised her eyebrows and gave her brother a quizzical look. "It's none of my business, but you probably should be home before Sally gets here."

Jeremy answered by walking out of the house and slamming the door.

Elizabeth Wakefield sat on her bed, pen and notepad on her lap, lost in thought. The article she was writing for *The Oracle*, Sweet Valley High's student newspaper, was giving her an unusual amount of trouble, and she was having a hard time concentrating.

Standing up to stretch, she wandered over to the window, eager for a distraction. As she scanned the shady, tree-lined street below, she saw Jeremy Larson ride by on his bike. His face looked like a thundercloud, and he was pedaling furiously.

She stared after him for a moment, lost in thought. After a few minutes, she felt refreshed enough to get back to her article. But shortly afterward, she heard the squeal of tires outside and a car door slamming. She shook her head. "Here comes Jessica," she said softly, an affectionate smile on her lips.

"Elizabeth!" Jessica Wakefield burst into her twin sister's room, panting after her dash through the house and up the stairs. She looked quickly from side to side and then ran to the window.

Elizabeth laughed. "What's wrong, Jess? Is somebody following you?"

Her sister whirled around to face her, her blond hair swirling around her shoulders. "It's an emergency!" she hissed.

"Oh?" Elizabeth wasn't alarmed. Her sister's emergencies were hardly ever more serious than an occasional lip-gloss shortage.

"What's happened this time? Some cute guy didn't look at you during cheerleading or something?"

Jessica folded her arms and looked at her twin imploringly. "Liz, you never take me seriously. Please, for once, will you believe me?"

Elizabeth took one look at her sister's serious expression and stopped smiling. She never meant to hurt her twin. Their special bond made it painful for her if her sister's feelings were hurt, even if Jessica didn't always seem to have the same regard for her. "I'm sorry, Jess, I was just teasing you. Really," she said. "What's wrong?"

Jessica squeezed her hands together and shifted her weight from one foot to the other. She was worried, anxious, and excited. "I've got—" Her blue-green eyes opened wide, and she burst out, "I brought home a puppy!"

Elizabeth's mouth dropped open in utter disbelief. "What? Jessica, you can't do that without asking Mom and Dad first!"

"I know," Jessica admitted, biting her lip. Then her face lit up with a brilliant smile. "But they won't even be back from that resort until Sunday night, and it might be too late then. Just come and look at him, Lizzie. A man had all these puppies in a box at the game, and he was just giving them away! He's the most adorable thing you ever saw. Really!"

"The man or the puppy?"

"Liz! The puppy!"

Elizabeth shook her head, smiling in spite of the seriousness of what Jessica had done. "But, Jessica, you don't even like dogs. Remember how much you hated taking care of Mrs. Bramble's dog?"

"Liz, that was ages ago. We were in sixth grade. I love dogs now."

Elizabeth's raised eyebrows should have conveyed some skepticism to Jessica. The episode with Mrs. Bramble had been a fiasco. Jessica, who had promised to take care of the old woman's dog, had tied it up, then sneaked away to a rock concert, and it had broken loose and run away. It was a miracle the incident had ended happily.

Now Jessica was looking at Elizabeth earnestly. "I really do love dogs now, honest. Especially this one."

"Jess, you've really outdone yourself this time."

"Oh, Liz, you're smiling. That means it's OK. Come on," she cried, grabbing her twin's hand and trying to pull her from the bed. "Please come look at him." She grinned. "I promise that if you don't absolutely adore him the minute you see him, I'll take him right back."

Elizabeth laughed. "OK, OK! You're dislocating my shoulder!" she teased, standing up.

"Oh, you're the most wonderful sister in the whole universe!" Jessica shrieked. She threw her arms around Elizabeth and then grabbed her hand again.

With Elizabeth in tow, Jessica raced down the stairs of the Wakefields' split-level home and out to the street. "There!" Jessica cried triumphantly, her arms extended.

At the curb was the girls' red Fiat convertible. Though it was a glorious day, the top was up. Elizabeth soon realized why. A pudgy little golden Labrador pup, tail wagging exuberantly, was standing on the passenger seat. His front paws rested on the window, which was open enough to allow him air.

Elizabeth stared, trying to take in every feature of the puppy at once. He had brown eyes and a healthy share of fat underneath his golden yellow fur. He seemed to be grinning with pure delight as he looked at the twins. Elizabeth was captivated.

"Ohhh," she murmured, opening the door. The puppy promptly fell out and then scrambled into her waiting arms as she sat down. He grunted and yipped in ecstasy as Elizabeth fondled his silky ears.

Her eyes shining, Elizabeth looked up at Jessica. "Oh, Jess, he's the most . . ." She looked down at the puppy squirming in her lap.

"I told you," Jessica said. She was grinning as she reached for the dog and folded him in her arms. "This is without question the most beautiful, lovable, adorable, darling, sweet— " She broke off breathlessly, out of words to describe him. "Puppy in the whole world," she concluded. She gave him a loud kiss.

"You're right," Elizabeth whispered. She couldn't take her eyes off the puppy. And she couldn't stop smiling.

A car drove past, reminding the girls that they should get their new dog inside.

"Now listen, Liz. I know I should have asked first," Jessica began, as she pushed the door open. "But since Mom and Dad are away for the weekend, I figured we could keep him and hide him, then show them after we've had him for a while." She turned innocent eyes on her sister. "Once they see he's no trouble, they'll say yes. I'm sure of it."

Elizabeth smiled skeptically. "No trouble, Jess? Is he housebroken?"

A momentary look of confusion crossed Jessica's face as they stood in the hallway. She looked at the puppy and bit her lip nervously. But she quickly recovered and widened her eyes. "Liz! How could you even think I'd bring an unhousebroken puppy into our home?" Her face took on a look of hurt innocence. "But just in case he can't wait," she added hastily, "maybe we'd better get some newspaper."

"Jessica! Are you sure he's housebroken? Or at least paper-trained?"

Jessica shrugged. "Oh, don't worry about it. He must be. Let's just be prepared—for emergencies or something."

"Hmmm. Yes, I think we'd better." Elizabeth eyed the puppy with a mixture of nervousness and tenderness. "You're such a doll, little puppy," she crooned as she tickled him under

11

his chin. "But what are we going to do with you?"

He looked up at her with adoring, luminous eyes. The girls laughed with delight.

"He'll stay in my room," Jessica stated firmly.

"But, Jess," Elizabeth warned. "He can't stay there when Mom and Dad get home. They'll find him."

Jessica hugged the puppy close. "I'll think of something, Liz. I will. Besides, no one ever goes in my room."

She was right about that, Elizabeth thought. Jessica's room usually looked like an earthquake zone, and Mrs. Wakefield had long ago given Jessica her last lecture on neatness. But even if someone did go in, anything as small as the puppy would probably be hidden under mounds of clothes.

"And I'll take such good care of him," Jessica added earnestly. "I really will."

Elizabeth shook her head. She had never seen Jessica so serious about taking on responsibility, but she was sure that keeping the puppy a secret from their parents would be utterly impossible. On the other hand, Jessica had pulled off a lot more outrageous stunts than this in the past. Elizabeth walked into the living room with Jessica behind her.

She tickled the puppy again. "Now you stay quiet and be on your best behavior, sweetheart."

"That's right," Jessica added, rocking him in

her arms like a baby. "Because we want to keep you right here with us."

In response to that, the pup squirmed out of Jessica's arms and landed on the floor, rolling into the coffee table. Elizabeth lunged forward to grab a vase of flowers just as it skidded across the slick surface to the edge, and Jessica tackled the dog before it could scurry into the hall. For one suspended moment, the two girls stared at each other, scarcely daring to breathe.

Then the dog yipped twice and licked Jessica's face. Both girls burst into laughter.

Two

"We're almost there, Sally. We'll be home in about five minutes."

Sally Larson smiled gratefully at her uncle Hal. *Home*, she echoed in her mind. Could she really be coming home at last? Could this beautiful, quiet town really be hers?

She settled back against the car seat and looked out the window at the beautiful California town. It seemed that each house was prettier than the last.

Whatever happens, please don't make me leave again, she prayed silently. *Please let me stay here. I want a home so much.*

Some of the places she had lived before could have been homes. But none of them had worked out. She knew it wasn't her fault. Some people just couldn't adjust to having a new person moving in with their families. But fault or no fault, she'd always had to leave, to move to yet another foster home.

They passed two little boys on bikes. The kids were laughing and calling out to each other in the dim early evening light, and a large, shaggy dog bounded happily along beside them. A sprinkler doused the car briefly as they drove past, and a man stood on his porch, smoking a pipe.

Sally pressed her lips together to keep them from trembling. *I'm going to make this work,* she vowed to herself. *I'll do anything, anything, to make Uncle Hal and Aunt Anne glad I came. And Dana and Jeremy, too,* she added.

What about Dana and Jeremy? she wondered. What would they be like? Would they like her? Would they be glad she'd come?

Before she had time for any more speculation, Mr. Larson pulled into the driveway and stopped the car. "Here we are, Sally," he said, smiling. "All set?"

Sally swallowed hard and bravely returned her uncle's smile. She couldn't even bring herself to look up at the house, afraid it would mysteriously disappear if she did.

"Hey, don't worry," he said, seeming to sense her nervousness. He tousled her hair and then gently lifted her chin with his finger. "You'll be just fine, Sally. Honest."

The flood of gratitude Sally felt almost overwhelmed her. But she didn't want her uncle

Hal to think she was a crybaby—or even worse, that she was unhappy about the arrangements— so she gritted her teeth. "OK, I guess—" she broke off, trying to gain control of her emotions.

"That's my girl. Let's go!"

Gripping her shoulder bag tightly, Sally followed her uncle up the slate walk to the front door. He opened it and then stepped aside to wave her through.

"Sally, I'm so glad you're here." An attractive woman stepped forward and kissed her on the forehead. "I'm your aunt Anne."

Sally, unused to any kind of affection, blushed, but she basked in the warmth of her aunt's tender smile. Her aunt looked much as she remembered her from years before and from photographs she'd seen.

"Hello," she managed to say in a subdued voice. "Thank you so much for inviting me."

"Oh, not at all! You're part of our family, Sally. And you remember that," Mrs. Larson chided. "And this is Dana."

Sally looked quickly in the direction her aunt indicated, almost expecting to see the same girl she had played with when they were kids. But standing in another doorway was a tall, leggy blond, whose pretty features were crowned by an outrageous hairstyle. She was wearing skin-tight, black stirrup pants and a gold lamé dinner jacket, sleeves pushed up, over a black- and white-checked shirt.

Dana flashed a brilliant smile. "Hi, Sally. It's really great to see you again."

For a moment, Sally was speechless. Was this chic, sophisticated girl, Dana? "Uh, hi," she stammered, suddenly feeling drab in her jeans and cardigan sweater. She looked around quickly. "Isn't—?"

Dana crossed her arms and rolled her eyes dramatically. "My dear brother Jeremy is late, as usual," she said with a grin. "But don't worry, you shouldn't be in too much of a hurry to meet him."

"Here we go!" Uncle Hal came back inside with a suitcase in each hand.

Sally stood in silence, trying to take everything in, the house, her aunt and uncle, and especially, Dana. She seemed so bright, so cool. She would almost be intimidating if she didn't also seem to be so friendly.

"Hey, why don't I show you your room?"

"Sure. Thanks."

Dana smiled again and picked up one suitcase. "It's this way."

As Sally followed her upstairs, Dana chattered. "Sweet Valley's a pretty good school, except for old Chrome Dome. That's Mr. Cooper, the principal. Man, can he be a drag! But we've got loads of good teachers, and all of the kids are great. You'll really like it. Anyway, this is it!"

Opening a bedroom door, Dana gestured grandly. "Your bedchamber, madam."

Sally giggled. "Thanks," she said, stepping inside. "Wow, this is really nice."

"You like it?" Dana bounded into the room and jumped on the bed. "It used to be Jerry's room, but he got moved up to the attic."

A stricken expression clouded Sally's face. "Oh, no! I don't want to put anybody out of their room or anything. I can sleep in the attic. Really."

Dana bounced on the mattress a few times, as if testing it. "Don't worry about it. He's a real grouch sometimes, but the attic is even better than this. Can I help you unpack?"

"Oh, no. I don't really have that much." Sally pointed at her two small suitcases.

"Then, I'll just stay and watch you unpack, OK?" said Dana.

The eager smile on Dana's face was too much to resist. Sally melted, delighted by her exuberant cousin. "Well, sure, if you really want to." She didn't want to seem rude or ungrateful, but she didn't want to be a bother.

"Great. So, anyway, what do you like to do?"

Sally shrugged, still shy. "I don't know, anything, I guess."

"Movies? I love old flicks. You know, the classics. Bergman, Bogart, Hitchcock . . ." Dana stretched luxuriously and sighed. "Ohhh, I love them. There's a great old theater in town, The Plaza. It's always got something good."

With a little nod, Sally looked at her cousin. "Sure," she said quietly. "I like movies."

"How about music? What sort of music do you like?"

Sally paused a moment as she was hanging up some blouses and skirts. "Well . . . I don't know," she said, turning around to face her cousin. "Anything, I guess." She colored slightly, thinking how dumb she must sound to Dana.

But her cousin didn't seem to notice. "Great. I'm in a band, you know. We're called The Droids. I'm the lead singer." Dana was lying face up on the bed, scissoring her legs back and forth above her.

Sally stared. *Wow! A singer in a band*, she thought. How could she ever impress somebody that sophisticated?

"And I told everybody I'd bring you to practice on Monday afternoon," Dana continued. "You could help out and stuff, too, if you want."

"Oh, uh, that's great," Sally said, using what seemed to be Dana's favorite word.

As Dana sat up, eyeing the contents of Sally's suitcase, all of Sally's old insecurities came back. She looked down at her conservative wardrobe, turtlenecks, oxford shirts, blue denim jeans, A-line skirts, a corduroy jumper. Then she glanced up quickly at her cousin's stylish clothes and haircut. She fingered her own brown shoulder-length hair nervously. It looked as if she would never fit in, she worried.

"Hey, listen, Sally, how about if I take you down to the Valley Mall tomorrow, and we can get you some new school clothes? I'm sure Mom would pay for it."

"Well . . ." Sally looked hesitant ly at the clothes spilled out on the bed. She blushed, realizing that Dana must think they were shabby. "I don't want to be a bother. I've got enough stuff for school."

"Oh, come on! How can you pass up this golden opportunity?"

Sally looked at Dana's eager face and then back down at the plaid skirt in her hands. She knew she didn't have the greatest clothes in the world, but at least she felt comfortable in them. And she didn't want her aunt to think she was asking for a whole lot as soon as she arrived. But Dana really seemed to want to.

"Are you sure?"

The look on Dana's face erased all doubt. "No problem. It'll be—"

"Great?" Sally supplied with a shy smile. She couldn't believe she and her cousin were getting along so well so soon.

Dana laughed freely. "You've got it!"

Downstairs, Mr. and Mrs. Larson heard the back door slam. They exchanged a quick glance.

"Is that you, Jerry?" Mrs. Larson called out. "We're in the den."

Jeremy slouched into the room and stood leaning against the wall. He eyed his parents warily. "Is Miss Neglected Child here yet?"

Mr. Larson heaved an exasperated sigh, obviously trying hard not to get mad. "Yes, she is," he said, his voice tight. "And I might add I'm a little disappointed you weren't here when she arrived."

Rolling his eyes, Jeremy pushed himself away from the wall and took a seat, staring fixedly at the television. "Sorry," he mumbled grudgingly.

"Jeremy! How can you be so—so inconsiderate of your cousin's feelings?" His mother shook her head angrily. "The least you could have done—"

"I said I was sorry, OK? Give me a break."

Mr. Larson stood up and turned off the television. He faced his son angrily. "No, it is not OK, and I will not give you a break. We're talking about my niece, your cousin, and I would appreciate, no, I insist—" he emphasized, fixing Jeremy with a steely glare. "I insist that you treat her with respect and courtesy. I don't expect you to like her immediately, but you can at least go say hello and welcome her into your room."

The two locked eyes for a tense moment.

"Do it."

"All right, all right! Jeez!" Jeremy stood up,

22

digging his hands in his pockets. He shrugged. "I'll do it. Satisfied?"

Mr. Larson regarded his son. "No, but it'll have to do for now."

"And so anyway, there's Max—we use his basement to practice in. He's the lead guitarist. And then— Oh, hi, Jeremy."

The two girls looked up from their positions sprawled on Sally's bed. Sally was slightly disturbed by the blank expression on Jeremy's face. It wasn't a scowl, certainly. But it sure wasn't a smile.

"Hi," she said with a tentative smile. "I'm Sally."

He nodded and looked over one shoulder. Then he glanced back at the girls. "Yeah. Hi. Like my room?"

Sally was stunned.

"Jeremy! You jerk, it's not your room anymore," Dana cried, jumping to Sally's defense.

"I'm sorry, Jeremy. I didn't mean for you to get kicked out on my account." Sally bit her lip. Things weren't getting off to such a hot start with Jeremy. She'd have to make a special effort to make him like her. "I'll switch with you, if you want."

Dana punched her. "Don't say that, dummy. He probably would." Then she stopped herself, seeing the look on Sally's face. "No, honest, he really wouldn't want to switch back now. Right, Jeremy?" She looked pointedly at her brother.

He met her gaze and then nodded slowly. "Yeah. I don't care."

There was an uncomfortable silence in the room for a moment. Sally looked down at her hands, wondering how on earth she could get around this bad first encounter with Jeremy.

Jeremy turned abruptly and headed for the attic.

Dana stared at the doorway for a moment longer, as if she expected him to reappear. Then she shook herself and drew a deep breath. "Boy, talk about the welcome wagon!"

She turned and looked quickly at Sally, whose head was still bowed.

"Hey, Sally, don't worry about him. He's always like that."

Sally looked questioningly into Dana's face. "You're not just saying that, are you?"

With a short laugh, Dana stood up. "I wish Jeremy was born a drag."

Sally squared her shoulders. She had no choice but to believe her cousin. Otherwise, it meant Jeremy already disliked her, and she couldn't let that happen.

Later, when Sally was finally in bed, she fought off sleep long enough to recapture the last few hours of her day. Sweet Valley was even more than she'd dreamed of, she thought. It was so pretty, and everyone seemed so nice and happy. Except Jeremy, she added to herself, a frown creasing her forehead. She hoped she didn't make him unhappy. Maybe Dana was right. Maybe Jeremy was just a grouch all the time.

She smiled again, thinking about Dana's eagerness to take her shopping. Even if she didn't want new clothes, Sally wouldn't pass up the chance in a million years. If that was what Dana wanted to do, then she'd do it. She'd do anything to make sure she was welcome in the Larson home.

Sally snuggled down into the covers. "Sheets never felt this good," she murmured sleepily. No bed was ever this comfortable. No other town was so beautiful.

Three

"Don't you think malls are wild? They're like the new Main Street, USA, know what I mean?" Dana took a bite of a soft pretzel and gave Sally a huge grin.

Sally looked around her at the colorful storefronts. Old ladies and young mothers with strollers sat on the benches by the fountain. "Yeah, I'm sure a lot of people come here just to watch other people."

"Exactly. OK. Let's hit Lisette's. We can definitely find stuff for you there."

Following Dana, Sally took a deep breath, trying to prepare herself mentally. Shopping with Dana would be fun, she realized. But she also had a feeling that her cousin would want her to buy things that weren't really Sally's style. She was even more sure of it when they

27

entered a store pulsing with music and filled with trendy clothing.

Sally stifled a sigh, glanced at her energetic, confident cousin, and came to a decision. If letting Dana pick out her clothes would help Dana accept her, Sally was ready to agree. She'd agree to anything to gain Dana's friendship.

"Oh, get this!" Dana cried, swooping down on a rack of jeans. She held out a pair of black denims, trying to judge how they would look on Sally. "Do you like them?"

"Yes, I do. Where do you try things on?" Sally looked around, feeling overwhelmed by the lights, colors, and music.

"Over there. And I'll look for more stuff while you're in there," Dana said, waving her on.

As Sally wandered off in search of the dressing rooms, she stared in amazement at the clothes around her. They were so offbeat—and expensive! She glanced at one price tag and shook her head in disbelief. She'd never been allowed to buy such expensive things. In fact, she had hardly ever bought new clothes. Most of what she had was hand-me-down stuff.

She closed the door of a cubicle, hurriedly pulled on the jeans, and studied her reflection in the mirror. They really weren't so wild, she decided. And she added firmly that she should dress more creatively, more like Dana. There was no reason to wear such boring clothes all the time.

"Sally, where are you?"

She jumped up, startled by Dana's voice. "In here."

Dana rattled the door. "Let me in."

Embarrassed, Sally unlatched the door to let her cousin into the tiny room. She wasn't used to having someone with her when she changed.

Dana's arms were laden with blouses, miniskirts, and pullovers in bright colors and patterns. "They're great." She turned her attention to the pile in her arms. "Try this," she commanded, pulling a pink sweatshirt out of the mess.

Sally took it without a word.

"And you can always pick up great things at thrift shops, too," her cousin continued. "And really cheap."

Turning away so Dana wouldn't see her burning face, Sally pulled on the sweatshirt. She'd had to buy lots of things at thrift shops over the years. And not because it was trendy.

"Let me see, let me see." Dana turned Sally around and surveyed her critically. Sally watched her cousin nervously as she was being examined. But all at once, Dana hugged her in a quick, affectionate embrace. "You look great, really."

A warm glow spread through Sally as her cousin beamed at her. It was heaven to be the center of Dana's attention. She was so lively, so spontaneous, so fun. Sally couldn't remember anyone ever making such a fuss over her before.

Overcoming her shyness, Sally returned the hug. "What else did you find?"

For the next few minutes the girls pored over the selection of clothes and made their decisions. Sally objected only once, when she realized how much it would all cost.

But Dana laughed away her worries. "Relax. Mom gave me her credit card. My folks are usually pretty strict with money, but every once in a while they let us go wild, you know?"

Although Sally had never been allowed to go "wild," she couldn't help catching Dana's high spirits, and decided to stop worrying. This seemed to be what Dana and her aunt wanted her to do, so she was happy to agree.

As they walked out of the store, she spoke up shyly. "Thanks, Dana, for helping me pick out these clothes. I've never had such a good time."

Dana paused for a moment, as if surprised. "No problem. I had fun, too."

Elizabeth glanced nervously over her shoulder as Jessica examined the dog collars. It was early for anyone they knew to be shopping, but it was still better to be cautious. At least the Perky Pet Shop was deserted. She looked back as Jessica spoke.

"How about those rhinestones? Aren't they cute?"

"Jess, don't you think it's a little tiny? You put that kind on a French poodle, not a Labrador."

"All right, all right. This one."

Elizabeth turned the brown studded collar over in her hands. "Hmmm. That's better."

"OK, then let's just get it and get out of here."

Jessica hurried to the cash register with the brown collar and a leash, and Elizabeth followed. After the night before, the collar had become their number-one priority. Their pudgy little pup was turning out to be a master escape artist. He could wriggle out of their grasp in a moment. Being able to tie him to something was important. At least that was what Elizabeth had insisted.

"I still think it's cruel to tie up a little baby like that." Jessica pouted as she turned away from the cashier, package in hand.

"Jess, it's not like we're going to bind and gag him. It's just for safety. What if he got loose and ran into the street?"

Jessica stopped and faced her sister with a look of horror on her face. "Don't even say such a thing!"

"OK." Elizabeth laughed. "Let's go."

"Wait a second!" commanded Jessica in a hoarse whisper as they walked out of the shop.

She grabbed Elizabeth's arm and held her back. "Maria Santelli and Sandra Bacon are over there. OK, they're gone. I wonder what they're doing at the mall so early?" she added.

Chuckling, Elizabeth began walking. "Talk about drama, Jess. You should be an actress."

"Elizabeth! Jessica! Wait up!"

The twins froze in their tracks, paralyzed by the voice calling their names. Turning around, Elizabeth saw Dana Larson and another girl walking toward them. She heard the paper bag rustle as Jessica whipped it behind her back.

"Hi, you guys," Dana called as she approached. She laid a hand on her companion's arm. "This is my cousin, Sally. She's just moved in with us."

Elizabeth smiled warmly at the pretty, dark-haired girl. "Dana told us you were coming. Welcome to Sweet Valley."

"Thanks," Sally answered, with a tentative smile of her own.

Elizabeth noticed the girl look from her to Jessica and laughed sympathetically. "Yes, we're identical twins."

"Oh, I didn't mean—" Sally began. She felt embarrassed that Elizabeth had noticed her staring at them. But it was hard not to stare, she thought. With their blond, shoulder-length hair, blue-green eyes and slender figures, they were both gorgeous.

Jessica tried to catch Elizabeth's eye. "It's re-

ally nice to meet you, but we've got to go now."
She started to back away, but Dana stopped
her.

"What are you being so mysterious about,
Jessica? What are you hiding?" she teased, cran-
ing her neck to see around Jessica.

"Nothing! Nothing at all. We're just in a hurry,
that's all!"

Dana wasn't giving up easily. "Come on, Jess,"
she said, folding her arms and tilting her head
to one side. "Now it's a challenge. I'm not
leaving you alone until you show me what
you've got."

Elizabeth could tell her sister was getting desperate. She turned and stared steadily into Jessica's blue-green eyes. "Go ahead, Jess. It's no
secret."

Jessica's eyes opened wider as she stared back
at her sister.

"Just show them. It's really a joke," she ex-
plained, turning to Dana and Sally with a laugh.
She took the bag and pulled out the dog collar.
"See?"

Dana's forehead creased with surprise. "I
didn't know you had a dog."

"Oh, we don't. It's for a costume. Right, Jess?"

Jessica relaxed visibly and reached for the
collar. "Isn't it outrageous?" she asked, putting
it around her own neck. "It's for a punk outfit.
You should wear one at a concert sometime,
Dana."

With a shrug, Dana laughed. "That's not a bad idea. Anyway, we've got to go. We have more shopping to do. See you on Monday."

Sally Larson, who had been silent, cast Elizabeth and Jessica a brief smile before turning away with her cousin. "It was nice meeting you."

"Sure. See you in school." As Elizabeth and Jessica watched them head for the other end of the mall, they both breathed a sigh of relief.

"Elizabeth Wakefield! You little con artist!" Jessica squealed, throwing her arms around her sister. "I never knew you had it in you!"

"Yeah, well, let's just get home so we don't have to go through that again, OK?"

Dana and Sally dropped their packages on Sally's bed. "Whew," Dana said, flopping down. "Talk about shopping fever."

She glanced over at her cousin, who was beginning to sort through the bags. Dana took in Sally's straight, shoulder-length hair with the middle part, her pale complexion, her sad eyes, and decided that clothes wouldn't be enough. Sally would need a new hairstyle, makeup, a whole new image.

"You know," Sally said, sitting down with a pair of new shoes in her lap. "This is so incredibly different from, well—" She broke off, searching for the right words. She faced Dana with a look of wonder on her face. "I've never lived in such a nice place before."

"Listen, forget about it, OK?" Dana said. "You live with us now, so you don't have to think about your old life. You can just pretend it never happened, right?" She paused, looking carefully at her cousin's face. "Right?" she insisted.

A look of surprise crossed Sally's features. "Oh, sure, I'll just try to forget about it."

There was an awkward pause as the two looked at each other. Dana wondered briefly if she had hurt Sally's feelings. But she decided it would really be better for everyone if Sally just forgot her past. It was so awful, she must want to.

"Listen, I've got a great idea!"

Sally's face brightened. For a moment, Dana felt guilty. Her cousin seemed so desperate to please her.

"How about if we do a makeover on you, huh? New life, new look, the works!" She beamed at Sally, suddenly impatient and eager for action. Her nature pushed her to go ahead and move.

Sally hesitated, then said, "All right. Thanks."

"OK, let's go to my room. Bring all your stuff so you can try it on."

Dana led the way into her own room, a sanctuary of old movie star posters and art prints, and yanked open bureau drawers. She threw hairbrushes, makeup, and costume jewelry onto her bed. Then she turned to Sally. "You sit there," she directed, pointing with a comb at a chair, "and we'll get to work."

Taking a long hard look at her cousin's face, Dana set to work skillfully with a can of styling mousse and a brush. "Would you mind if I cut your hair just a little?" she asked with a hopeful smile.

Sally hesitated a moment.

"Nothing outrageous. I promise!"

With an uncertain smile, Sally nodded. "Sure. My hair's totally boring anyway. Go ahead!

"Elizabeth and Jessica seemed really nice," Sally said a few minutes later, wincing under the force of Dana's hairstyling. "They're really pretty. But how can you tell them apart?"

Dana shrugged. "I don't know. You just do. After you've known them for a while, you will, too. You should have seen Jessica a couple of weeks ago. She dyed her hair black for some bizarre reason. Then there was no way you could mix them up. Hold still, all right?" She was enjoying taking control and didn't want to talk about anyone else.

They were silent for a few moments. Dana was focusing all her energy on Sally's hair and face. She had a vague, almost unconscious, desire to have Sally look up to her, to think of her as a role model. She would help Sally with clothes and makeup, introduce her to the right people, influence her taste in music, movies, and books.

By the time she was through, Sally would be a whole new person.

Then Sally spoke again. "I'm really excited about going to school on Monday. I feel like for once I'll be staying." She sighed and shifted slightly on the chair. "None of my other schools ever felt right, you know? I always knew I'd end up having to leave."

Behind Sally's back, Dana scowled. She was concentrating on creating a new Sally, but Sally insisted on bringing up the past. "Listen, I really think you should think about the future. And also," she added, coming around in front of Sally, "you should probably tell people you're sixteen. That way they won't know you had to stay back a grade."

She looked intently into Sally's face, searching for signs of agreement. After a moment, Sally dropped her eyes to her lap, and nodded. "If you say so, Dana."

With a sigh of relief, Dana nodded. *Why complicate life?* she told herself firmly, ignoring the little twinge of embarrassment she felt about Sally's past. "I think it's really the best thing to do."

Four

"How about Spot?" Jessica asked. It was Sunday afternoon, and she was sitting on the kitchen floor by the puppy.

"Spot? Are you kidding? He doesn't have any spots, you dope."

"I know. That's why it's such a good name."

Elizabeth chuckled and turned away from the counter. She set a bowl of Puppy Chow down on the floor. The still-nameless puppy sniffed eagerly at the bowl and began to eat.

Taking a seat on the floor by her twin, Elizabeth watched the dog fondly. A shaft of late-afternoon sunshine slanted through one plant-filled window and lit the puppy's golden fur. "Why don't we give him a real name. It's more dignified."

"Good idea," Jessica said, her expression thoughtful. "Such as?"

Elizabeth thought for a moment. "Hmmm. How about something regal, something like . . ." She paused, looking into space. "How about Prince Albert? What do you think of that?"

Her sister considered it, stroking the puppy's ears. "Prince Albert," she said experimentally. "Yeah. I like it. Prince Albert. Your Highness." She giggled, bowing to the puppy.

He looked up and wagged his tail. Jessica looked up at the ceiling. "You know, I can't stand keeping this a secret." She looked at Elizabeth hopefully.

"Huh-uh, Jess. No way. We agreed."

"Not even Jeffrey?" Jessica asked with an arch smile.

A blush colored Elizabeth's tanned cheeks. She still felt that special rush of pleasure whenever she thought of handsome, blond Jeffrey French.

He had moved to their California town from Oregon recently and had caused quite a sensation among the Sweet Valley High girls. At first, Elizabeth wasn't interested in dating him. Eventually, though, he had won her over with his sincerity and charismatic personality.

It would be hard for her to keep a secret from Jeffrey. "OK," she conceded with a grin. "I'll probably tell Jeffrey and Enid. But only because I trust them completely, and I hate to hide anything from them." Enid Rollins was Elizabeth's best friend.

Jessica shrugged. "Are you trying to tell me I can't trust my friends?" One look from Elizabeth and she knew the answer. "All right, so maybe Lila and Cara have big mouths."

Their eyes met suddenly as the same thought occurred to both of them. "Oh, God," Elizabeth groaned. "Don't tell Cara, whatever you do. She'll tell Steve, and that'll be it."

Cara Walker was one of Jessica's best friends. She dated the twins' brother, Steven, who was a freshman in college. One word to Cara, and their parents would know about Prince Albert in less than five minutes. This puppy was something to keep from her.

"OK, I'll just tell Lila—and don't worry, I've got enough on her so she'll keep it a secret," Jessica said. "Hey, I guess he's finished dinner," she added, looking at Prince Albert again.

The chubby puppy sniffed at her shoulder and licked her, gazing up at her with adoring eyes. "As long as we can convince Mom and Dad that having a dog is no problem, we can keep you," she told him, rolling him over and tickling his belly.

Just then they heard a car pulling into the driveway.

"It's them!"

"They're home!"

In their hurry to remove the traces of Prince Albert's dinner, the girls relayed their panic to the puppy. As Elizabeth turned to pick him up, she saw a puddle spreading on the floor beneath him. "Oh, no!" she cried.

"Give him to me!" Jessica screeched. She reached over to scoop him up, stood up, turned on her heel, and ran through the house.

"Girls? Where are you?"

When Ned and Alice Wakefield entered the kitchen through the back door, Elizabeth was on her knees on the floor mopping up the mess.

"Hi, sweetheart," her mother said, putting down her purse. "Spill something?"

Her face burning, Elizabeth nodded. Trust Jessica to leave her with the dirty work. "Uh, yeah."

Mr. Wakefield set down their small suitcases. "Where's Jess?"

"Here I am. Hi, Mom. Hi, Dad," said Jessica, breezing through the door her parents had just entered. She kissed them both. "Have a good time? We were so bored this weekend. We didn't do anything at all. Did we?"

Throwing the last sopping paper towel into the garbage, Elizabeth turned to her sister with a question in her eyes. "That's right." She held her sister's gaze, dying to ask her where Prince Albert was, but Jessica turned away.

"How was Casa de los Caballos? Did you have fun?"

Alice Wakefield, whose pretty, youthful face often led people to think she was the twins' older sister, breathed a contented sigh. She

42

smiled at her husband. "I'd say we had a lovely time."

Ned Wakefield returned her smile. "Yes, we—"

"Well, that's great," Jessica interrupted. "I've got homework. See you later." She turned abruptly and left the kitchen.

"Me, too," Elizabeth said and, ignoring her parents' surprised looks, she followed her sister out into the hall. "Where is he?" she whispered hoarsely as they reached the stairs.

Jessica paused, one hand on the banister. "He's in my room."

"Jess, this is crazy. It'll never work."

Jessica tossed her golden hair back over her shoulders and said with an air of supreme confidence, "Don't worry, I've got everything under control."

Rolling her eyes, Elizabeth muttered, "That's exactly what I'm afraid of."

On Monday afternoon, Sally shut her locker and leaned against it, completely exhausted. Class schedules, new teachers, finding rooms, her locker combination—her head was spinning from all the things she had to keep track of. On top of that, she figured she must have met every student at Sweet Valley High, and she knew she would never remember all their names. Meeting new people was something she'd had to do all her life, and she was never very good at it. Somehow, when she knew she might never see them again anyway, it was hard to absorb faces and names.

It was especially difficult that day, though, when she felt so unlike herself. She looked down at her clothes. They just weren't her, she decided. No wonder she felt so uncomfortable.

"There you are. Ready to go? Max is waiting for us outside."

Sally turned to see her cousin striding up to her, looking as full of energy as she had first thing in the morning. Dana was wearing a red miniskirt and a long gray cardigan sweater over a yellow shirt. They looked perfect for her.

"Did I meet Max?" Sally asked, searching her memory for a face to fit that name.

Dana took her arm. "No, not yet. He's in The Droids, remember? We're going to his house to practice."

Stopping uncertainly, Sally said, "Oh, I thought I'd just go home, Dana. Is that OK? I'm so tired."

Dana's face fell. "But, Sally, I told everyone I'd bring you today. They all want to meet you."

Sally bit her lip, trying to decide what to do. She was truly exhausted, and just wanted to go home and relax. And furthermore, she wasn't really interested in rock music. Being part of a band wasn't exactly her idea of fun.

On the other hand, Dana looked so disappointed. And one thing Sally didn't want to do was cause any problems between Dana and her. So if going to The Droids' rehearsal was what Dana wanted, Sally was willing to do it.

She remembered a girl she had known at a group home, where she'd had to stay once between foster homes. That girl, Marybeth, had told Sally, "When I get a good thing, I'm going to hang on with all I've got." *Hang on with all I've got,* Sally repeated to herself. *That's what I've got to do.* She managed a smile.

"Well, in that case, sure. I'm really excited about meeting all of them."

"Oh, good. You'll like everybody. I know it. Come on."

Twenty minutes later they were all in Max Dellon's basement, and Sally was meeting the rest of The Droids.

"Do you play an instrument, Sally?" Emily Mayer asked, offering her a can of soda.

"Well, no. I don't. Thanks." Sally looked apologetically at Dana and took a sip. "I never had a chance to learn."

"You could sing backup vocals, couldn't you?" Dana put in hurriedly.

Sally realized immediately that Dana didn't want her to explain why she'd never had the chance to learn, didn't want her to tell The Droids what kind of life she'd been leading. She shook her head, hoping she wasn't blushing. It wasn't as if she had been a criminal or a drug addict or anything. And it wasn't her fault either. But she suddenly felt ashamed anyway. "No, I can't sing either. Sorry."

"Hey, I know. You can sort of be our manager. We need one, guys, right?" Dana turned to her friends, obviously wanting them to accept Sally.

Guy Chesney shrugged. "I guess so. It's OK with me. You can help arrange our gigs, Sally. And just sort of help out, you know?"

Nodding eagerly, Sally agreed. "Sure, I'd be glad to. That is, if no one minds. I mean, don't you already have someone to do that?"

Dan Scott laughed. "We did have a professional manager once, but what a joke that turned out to be! He kept promising and promising but he didn't deliver. He wasn't really interested in the band."

"Let's not get into that, OK?" Dana said impatiently, running a hand through her blond hair. "It's no big deal. We just need someone sensible to keep track of dates, that's all. So we don't double book."

Sally nodded again, eager to please. "Sure, I can do that."

"Let's get started then, huh?" Dan threw his soda can into a basketball hoop over the garbage can. "And he scores! Let's go."

As The Droids started tuning up to begin practice, Sally sat back and thought about being the band's manager. No one had ever asked her to be part of any kind of group before, and it felt great. She just hoped she could learn to like their music.

Maybe liking music was just a matter of practice. Just listening to The Droids a lot would make her enjoy it more, she told herself firmly.

Guy struck a jangling chord on the keyboards and then another. "You know," he announced, sitting back and crossing his arms. "We need some new material. We've got to write some new songs."

"Like what?"

He shrugged. "I don't know. Throw out some ideas."

"Love! Death! Existential struggle!" Emily intoned dramatically, rattling out a drumroll. "Agriculture!"

"Yeah, right!" Max laughed. "Next?"

Sally grinned, watching the playful interaction between friends. She noticed Dana nodding her head as she considered an idea.

"How about 'The Ballad of Maria and Michael'?" she suggested, looking from one player to another. "It'd be hot stuff."

"Give me a break!" Dan begged, shaking his head in disgust. "Those two are a real pair of idiots."

With a start, Sally realized she knew whom, they were talking about. Dana had pointed out the two in school that day. A cheerleader named

Maria Santelli was dating a senior named Michael Harris, and apparently their parents didn't know and weren't supposed to know. It was a big secret. Dana said she'd heard there had been a bad business deal between the two fathers sometime in the past, and the families were supposed to be bitter enemies. Dana had laughed the whole thing off, but apparently it was the hottest gossip at Sweet Valley High.

Dana shrugged. "Sure, but we could really play up the drama, you know, Romeo and Juliet stuff."

The others joked about it for a few moments, until Emily spoke up. "Hey, wait a minute. How about a song named 'Romeo and Juliet'? I mean, forget Maria and Michael. The Romeo and Juliet story is still pretty powerful."

Within minutes, the group came to an agreement, and they all began picking out chords, trying different melodies, and tossing out lyrics. A spirit of excitement swept through The Droids as their new song took shape.

Sally was fascinated. She was actually watching the band come up with an idea and expand it into a song. A touch of melancholy invaded her thoughts as she realized that it was just the creative process that was interesting to her. She just couldn't take any interest in the song itself.

She noticed a pile of sheet music on the table next to her. The pages had the names of different band members at the top, so it was easy enough to sort them. Soon she had five neat piles of songs. And nothing else to do. With a sigh of resignation, she sat back again to listen. The band was running through some of their old material now, and since most of their songs were original, she didn't know any of them. To pass the time, she read through the words of some of the songs. Then she sat back again.

It was no use, she decided. She would never really be part of the band. She knew they'd probably accept her for Dana's sake. But that was about as far as it would go.

She let her thoughts wander. Her guidance counselor had mentioned a school newspaper—*The Oracle*, was it? That was something Sally would have liked to work on. Having been alone so much of her life, Sally had found comfort in writing. Her stories and poems were the only friends she could keep when she moved. But if she had to come to The Droids' practices two or three times a week, it didn't look as if she'd have time for the newspaper, too.

"Hey, Sally? Do you see a sheet of music that says 'Monterey Way' on it?" Dan leaned over the table, looking for the music. "Wow, did you just sort these? That's great." He found the sheet he was looking for in the pile with his name on it and flashed her an appreciative grin. "Thanks a lot."

As he reached to his guitar, Sally felt her heart pounding in her chest. Suddenly, she felt like one of them, and it was wonderful. And she also felt a new sense of urgency: No matter what, she couldn't do anything to jeopardize this new life. If she had to leave Sweet Valley now, she thought she would just die.

Five

"So how was your first day at Sweet Valley High, Sally? Did you like it?"

Sally nodded and swallowed. "It's really nice, Uncle Hal. But I'm afraid I'll never remember everybody's name."

"Don't worry about that now," Mrs. Larson said reassuringly. She looked at her children as she passed a bowl of salad. "I'm sure Dana and Jeremy can help you out whenever you need it."

Dana poured herself a glass of milk and turned her warm brown eyes on Sally. "Sure, no problem. Right, Jeremy?"

Sally looked quickly across the table at her cousin. Since she'd arrived on Friday night, he had hardly spoken a dozen words to her. She decided that having to give up his room had made him dislike her, but she vowed to make it up to him, no matter what. She smiled as he looked up and met her gaze.

"Yeah, right," he mumbled through a mouthful of baked potato.

Sally frowned, wishing she could get through to him, but not knowing how. She decided to concentrate on the rest of the family first. Maybe Jeremy would loosen up with time. "This pot roast is delicious, Aunt Anne. You're such a good cook."

Mrs. Larson touched her napkin to the corners of her mouth and smiled appreciatively. "That's sweet of you, dear. Do you cook at all?"

"Oh, I can make hamburgers and things like that. But nothing very good," Sally confessed.

"Well, I'd be glad to show you how if you're interested."

"I'd love it if you would, Aunt Anne. If it's not too much trouble," Sally hastened to add. Out of the corner of her eye, she saw Jeremy's scowl darken further. *Now what did I do?* she worried.

"Of course not, Sally. Don't be silly," Mrs. Larson replied. "I've tried to teach Dana, but she isn't interested in any aspect of cooking besides the eating part."

"And she's good at that," Mr. Larson teased, sending his daughter a wink.

Dana made a sour face.

"I think Dana's good at everything," Sally offered, smiling eagerly at her cousin. "I really enjoyed hearing her sing this afternoon. And

I'm so glad they're letting me be part of the band."

"I'm just OK," Dana said modestly. But Sally could tell she was pleased.

Sally sat back for a moment, relishing the last of her dinner. Everything about this new life so far was perfect—well, almost. She just had to try a little harder to make Jeremy like her. But the Larsons' home was so nice, and so comfortable. She looked at her uncle and aunt and thought how wonderful it must be for Dana and Jeremy to have two such wonderful parents. She was going to make them glad they'd asked her to stay.

"Well, whose turn is it to clear the table?"

Sally put down her fork hastily. "I'll do it."

"Wait a minute. It's Dana's turn," Jeremy spoke suddenly, sitting up straighter in his chair and turning to his mother. "Sally shouldn't be doing Dana's jobs! It isn't fair!"

"But I don't mind," Sally insisted. "I want to. Please?" Pushing her chair back, Sally began stacking dishes and taking them to the kitchen. Was that the problem? she wondered. Was Jeremy mad at her because she wasn't doing any of his chores? Sally made a mental note to take out the garbage before she went to bed to save him the trip.

On the way back she overheard Mrs. Larson say, "Well, I just can't get used to someone

53

actually volunteering to do anything in this house."

Dana looked up as Sally entered, a guilty smile on her face. "I can't just sit here while you do my job, Sally. I'll help."

"Oh, no! Please," Sally cried urgently. "That TV show you wanted to watch is starting now. Go on."

Dana looked at her mother and then back at Sally. "Are you sure you don't mind?"

"I'm positive."

Dana shrugged. "All right. Come on in and watch with us when you're done."

"I will," Sally replied, taking more dishes. She returned to the kitchen, feeling as though she'd scored a hit. *Just keep doing this*, she told herself. *Be helpful and they won't get rid of you.*

As soon as she had loaded and started the dishwasher, Sally cleaned up the kitchen and took the garbage out. Then, finding the family watching TV in the den, she took a seat on the sofa next to Dana.

"Anne, did the evening paper come yet?" Mr. Larson asked, settling into his favorite chair.

Sally jumped up again. "I saw it in the kitchen, Uncle Hal. I'll get it for you."

"Oh, no, Sally, you don't have to."

But Sally was already out the door.

"Well, thank you very much," Mr. Larson said as she brought the newspaper back. "That's very kind of you."

Sally smiled gratefully and sat back down again, thinking that if things continued this well, she'd have a permanent home at last. Dana sent her a grin, and they continued watching television for a while.

When the program was over, Jeremy started flicking through the channels with the remote control.

"Why don't you ask Sally what she'd like to see, Jeremy?" Mrs. Larson suggested, looking up from her needlepoint. She gave her son a meaningful look.

With exaggerated politeness, Jeremy turned to Sally. "Is there something you would like to watch now?"

Upset by the hostility in Jeremy's eyes, Sally felt herself blush. "No—no," she stammered, not wanting to anger him further. "Whatever you want to watch is fine with me. Honest."

He glared at her for a moment longer and selected a channel.

Filled with worry, Sally stared unhappily at the screen. Nothing she said or did was right when it came to Jeremy. She'd just have to try harder. But there was no telling what would work and what wouldn't.

"By the way, Sally. I want you to feel free to use my car whenever you need to," Mrs. Larson said.

Sally jumped. "Oh, thank you, Aunt Anne."

"Great, all we need is someone else to hog the car!"

"Jeremy! Sally is part of this family, too, with the same privileges you have." Mr. Larson looked at his son over the top of his newspaper. "And I might stress that they are privileges, not rights. Sally will use the car when she wants it."

Sally, who had watched the interaction between Jeremy and her uncle in shocked silence, spoke up quickly. "But I really won't want to use the car at all. I don't have anyplace to go, anyway. Really, Jeremy. I won't."

He grunted in reply, looking fixedly at the television set.

"Ignore him," Dana whispered, leaning close. "He's in a total antisocial phase right now. I'd like to do us all a favor and put him out of his misery."

Sally wanted to laugh, but didn't dare.

"Who can watch TV with everybody talking, anyway? I'm going upstairs." Jeremy pushed himself out of his chair and stalked out.

Dana shrugged and turned to the television set again.

"I swear I don't know what's gotten into him these days," Mrs. Larson complained, shaking her head. "I've never seen him be such a grouch."

Sally swallowed hard. "I think it's my fault, for taking his room."

"No—" Mrs. Larson began.

"Don't be ridiculous, Sally," Mr. Larson said, cutting off his wife. "It was our idea for you to use that room, not yours. Jeremy's really better off. He has more space and more privacy. And you girls are closer together. What's more, you are welcome in this home by all of us. Don't ever think otherwise. Dana and Jeremy will both be glad to do whatever they have to to make you comfortable, just as your aunt and I will."

Staring glumly at her lap, Sally nodded. She was trying not to cry. "I think I'll go upstairs now," she said hoarsely. "I've got homework to do." Meeting her aunt's eyes, she added, "Thanks for everything."

Mrs. Larson smiled tenderly and stood up, coming close to kiss Sally's cheek. "Of course, Sally. But from now on don't say 'thank you' anymore. All right?" She stayed there for a moment, her hands on Sally's shoulders.

Sally nodded, hardly daring to look into her aunt's kind face. She managed a brave smile. "All right," she said. Then squaring her shoulders, she turned and left the room.

Mr. and Mrs. Larson both stared at the doorway after Sally had left. Dana looked up to see them exchange a smile.

"Well," Dana's mother said brightly, sitting down with her needlepoint again, "she certainly is a nice girl, isn't she?"

Dana shrugged. "Sure."

"She's so helpful, too. I've never ever seen anyone so generous with her time. You know she would have done the breakfast dishes if I hadn't told her she'd be late for school."

Mr. Larson stretched and yawned. "She's a good kid, all right," he said, looking pointedly at his daughter. "And never complains a bit. Although God knows she's got a right to complain, the way she's been kicked around. You could learn a thing or two from her, Dana."

A strange thump in her chest made Dana frown. "I never knew you were dissatisfied with me before," she said with a twinge of sarcasm.

"Oh, Dana. We're not dissatisfied with you. You know perfectly well that's not what I meant. I'm just saying that Sally is a very generous, helpful girl, and a pleasure to have around. That's all."

Dana stared woodenly at the TV. "Well, it sure sounds like you're comparing me to her, and I'm coming up short."

Mr. Larson folded his newspaper, gave an exasperated sigh, and ran a hand through his graying hair. "Don't be childish, Dana. Of course we're not comparing you."

"Oh, and, Dana," Mrs. Larson put in, "I hope you aren't going to get in the habit of letting Sally do your chores for you. I don't want you to take advantage of her generosity."

"But, Mom! She wants to!"

"Dana, she's being polite!"

Speechless, Dana stared at her parents.

"Your mother's right, Dana. I don't want you to be selfish about it."

Dana sat in silence, watching the TV but not really seeing it. Normally, Dana prided herself on being an even-tempered person, slow to pass judgment. But this was too much! she thought angrily.

All weekend Sally had been doing nice little favors for Dana, offering to get her a snack while she was up, cleaning up their shared bathroom, clearing or setting the table for her, asking her opinion, and paying compliments.

At first, Dana had thought it was sweet of Sally, and flattering, too. Not to mention that it was nice not to have any household chores to worry about. Now it was starting to rankle a bit. She scowled suddenly. *Where do they get off comparing us, anyhow?* she thought angrily. Her parents kept telling her, "Be nice to Sally. Let her do what she wants." So if Sally wanted to clear the table, fine. But Dana didn't know they would turn around and start criticizing her for it.

"I'm going up to my room," Dana said suddenly, getting up from the couch. Without saying good night to her parents, she walked out of the den, leaving them staring after her.

Six

The door bell rang as Sally was coming down the stairs.

"I'll get it," she called over her shoulder.

She opened the door to face a tall, dark-haired boy who had an athletic build. With an uncertain, but friendly, smile, he stepped forward.

"Hi. Uh, is Jeremy here?" he asked, obviously confused about who she was, but smiling all the same. "I'm Mark Riley."

Sally responded to his easygoing politeness with her own smile and put out her hand. "I'm Sally Larson, Jeremy's cousin. I think Dana introduced us as we were passing in the hall yesterday."

Mark's eyes widened. "Oh, right!" he exclaimed, nodding as he shook her hand. "I guess I didn't recognize you."

With a start, Sally realized why. On both

Monday and Tuesday she had worn her new clothes to school. That afternoon she had changed into an old pair of jeans and an oxford shirt and had washed off the makeup Dana had helped her apply. She felt more comfortable that way. But she was surprised to find what a difference it made in her total appearance.

Mark Riley was still holding her hand and smiling at her, and she felt a rush of pleasure. "I'll get Jeremy," she stammered. "I think he's in the kitchen."

She turned toward the back of the house, and Mark followed her, keeping up an easy banter. "So how do you like Sweet Valley?" he asked. "Is this your first time in California?"

"No, I've lived in California all my life, up around San Francisco, mostly." Sally turned and looked back at him as she pushed open the kitchen door, angry and sorry that she had to conceal her past. "But I love it here," she added softly. "I'd hate to have to leave."

"Why would you have to leave?"

"Hey, Mark!" came Jeremy's voice.

"Hi, Jeremy! What's up?" As Mark entered the kitchen, he pushed Sally forward gently so that she entered, too. She couldn't tell whether he was just pushing her out of the way or wanted her to come in with him. She paused in the doorway, not knowing whether to stay or go.

"We're going to a game," Jeremy said, looking across the room at her. He might just as well have said, "And I don't want you here."

Flustered and hurt, Sally turned to go. "It was nice meeting you, Mark. See you in school."

"Hey, relax, where are you going?" Mark gave Jeremy a lopsided grin before speaking to Sally again. "Why don't you hang around? We're not leaving for a few minutes."

"Mark, we'd better take off pretty soon, you know." Jeremy's voice was low, but Sally could hear him anyway.

"What's the hurry?" Mark said, helping himself to a glass of apple juice. "It doesn't start for another hour."

Sally looked from one boy to the other. Mark was smiling at her, and Jeremy was looking steadily at a sports magazine spread out before him on the counter. Hesitantly, she sat down and took an apple from the fruit bowl.

"So," Mark continued, sitting across from her. "What classes do you have? Maybe I can save you some headaches."

She laughed. "What's that supposed to mean?"

"Well, for instance, do you have Mr. Fellows for history?" She nodded, amused. "Take it from me, he loves to get typed papers. I'm convinced it's worth about six and a half points on your grade."

"How about Mr. Frankel?" Sally teased. "Does he like math assignments typed, too?"

Mark spread his hands out, an expression of

mock dismay on his face. "Hey, what's with the abuse? I'm just trying to help!"

"Oh, I beg your pardon! Please go on."

After finishing off his juice, Mark launched into a humorous story about the math teacher. Sally listened eagerly, feeling a warm glow spread over her.

As he continued talking, Sally knew that Mark was attracted to her. And since his familiarity with the house meant he was a good friend of Jeremy's, maybe she could win Jeremy's friendship through Mark. She smiled happily, feeling that maybe things really would work out after all.

"And then he said, 'Please pass the tests to the front,' in this really embarrassed voice," Mark was saying, speaking to Sally and apparently ignoring his friend. "He couldn't believe he had given us the same test from the week before. It was a riot."

"But why didn't anyone say anything?"

Mark shrugged, a mischievous gleam in his eyes. "No talking during tests, right? That's the rule."

Sally grinned. She glanced at her cousin to see what he thought of his best friend's story. But her smile quickly faded. Jeremy was glaring at her through narrowed eyes. This time there was no mistaking his message. As the color rushed to her cheeks, Sally stood up, all her giddy elation gone. "I—I've got homework to do," she stammered, hurt and confused. She walked quickly to the door.

"Hey, wait a minute!" Mark cried, hopping off his stool. He paused awkwardly, as if embarrassed by his sudden outburst. "Sure you don't want to go to the game with us?"

Sally's heart gave a painful thump. *Of course!* she wanted to scream. *Of course I do. But Jeremy doesn't want me to, and I can't make anyone mad at me now!*

But she didn't. She looked quickly at Jeremy and lowered her burning eyes to the tile floor.

"She said she had homework, man. Let's go!"

Mark looked questioningly from Sally to Jeremy and back again.

"Yeah, I really do," Sally whispered, hardly trusting herself to meet his gaze.

He frowned and shrugged. "OK, if you say so. See you in school, all right?"

Sally pushed open the door and paused for a moment, her eyes closed. "Sure. 'Bye." Then she walked out and ran quickly up to her room, shutting out the sound of the front door slamming.

Jessica slammed the front door of the Wakefield home and dropped her books on the floor. She paused for a moment, listening to see if anyone was home. She didn't hear a sound.

"Come on," she said, grinning at her friend.

"Wait till you see him. You will absolutely die. But remember, whatever you do, don't tell Cara, or anybody else!"

Lila Fowler tossed her perfectly styled hair back and set an expensive handbag down on a nearby chair. "Don't get so hyper about it, Jessica. Where is he, anyway? I mean, how can you keep him a secret from your parents?"

"He's in the basement. I keep him down there during the day because there's lots of room to run around. And then I walk him and sneak him up to my room before Mom and Dad get home from work. He's paper-trained so I don't have to walk him at night. The only problem is, I can't get him into the basement in the mornings until after my parents leave for work. So I got to school late today."

Lila sent her friend a bitter smile as they headed for the basement stairs. "I could probably get ten puppies and sit them around the dining room table, and my dad wouldn't even notice."

Lila Fowler's father had made a fortune in the computer industry and was constantly away on business, leaving his daughter alone in their big mansion. He lavished everything on Lila: money, clothes, a flashy green sports car. Everything, in fact, except attention and love. Most of the time Lila was left in the care of the servants, but she had stopped listening to them years ago.

Jessica glanced over her shoulder as she started

down the basement steps. She smiled. "He's probably sleeping. Come on."

As they reached the bottom step and passed the laundry room, Prince Albert came bounding toward them, stumbling over his legs in his excitement. He landed in a heap at Jessica's feet and looked up at her lovingly.

"Hi, baby," she crooned, kneeling down to rub his ears.

"Did you really just get him from some stranger?" Lila asked, a slightly disdainful note in her voice. "I mean, he obviously can't be a purebred dog. He didn't have any papers, did he?"

"No, but who cares?" Jessica replied. "A dog doesn't have to be expensive to be nice," she added.

Lila sniffed. "Oh, I don't know. I'd rather be sure of what I was getting. Bloodlines are so important."

With an impatient shrug, Jessica turned her attention back to the squirming puppy at her feet. Lila and her bloodlines. Who needed them? "Did little baby have a nice day? Did you have fun playing?"

Prince Albert panted happily, and Lila stooped down to touch his fur, her expression suddenly much softer.

"He's so soft," Lila murmured. "He's really adorable."

"I know. I love him." Jessica scooped Prince

Albert into her arms and sat down with him in her lap. "We've had him since Friday night and so far, no problems," she said airily, looking up at her friend. "A few more days like this and I can show him to my parents. It'll prove that a dog won't be too much trouble."

Lila nodded, fondling the puppy. "You're so lucky," she said wistfully.

Jessica looked up at her friend in surprise. That didn't sound like the same Lila who was putting on airs a minute earlier.

"Well, anyway, Jess, I've got to go. I'll see you tomorrow." As she got up, Lila paused for a moment, staring at a dark corner of the basement. "Hey, Jessica, what's that?"

"What?"

"Over there. It looks like a snake."

"Oh, God, you're kidding," Jessica said nervously, peering into the corner. She looked at Lila. "It's not moving."

"Well, go see what it is!"

"OK, OK! Don't push me!" Squaring her shoulders, Jessica walked forward slowly, keeping her eyes riveted on the long black shape. With each step she became more and more sure it wasn't a snake, but she couldn't tell what it was. She stooped down and picked up a two-foot length of black rubber tubing. "Well, where did that come from?" she muttered, walking back with it to Lila.

Prince Albert yipped suddenly, wagging his

tail with excitement as he looked at the tubing in her hand. A sudden, sick sensation overcame Jessica, and she looked back at Lila, her eyes wide. "You don't think?"

Lila examined the piece of rubber, a skeptical look on her pretty face. "I wouldn't know, but those look a lot like tooth marks."

"Oh, God! What have you done?" Jessica wailed, looking frantically around her. "Where did this come from?" she asked, waving the tubing in Prince Albert's face. "Where did you get this?"

He wagged his tail.

"Come on, we've got to figure out where he got this."

For the next few minutes, Jessica and Lila searched the basement, trying to find something the piece of hose could have been attached to.

"Jess, come in here."

Feeling absolutely ill, Jessica followed Lila's voice into the laundry room. "Don't tell me. Please don't tell me."

Shaking her head, Lila turned to Jessica. "Look at the back of the washing machine, Jess. I think that's where he got it."

Inspection revealed that the tube had indeed been pulled and chewed from the back of the machine. Jessica leaned back against the dryer and groaned.

"What am I going to do?"

"Well, if I were you," Lila said, heading for the stairs, "I'd call a repairman. Soon." She put one foot on the bottom step. "But you've got to do it without me. I've got to go. 'Bye."

Jessica stayed where she was for a minute, glaring after Lila. *Trust her to leave when the going gets tough*, she fumed. *Some friend.* She looked up again and saw a furry little face looking around the corner at her.

"Oh, you little monster!" She sighed. "What are you trying to do to me?"

Prince Albert wagged his tail again and wiggled forward, as if asking for her forgiveness. Jessica picked him up, then ran lightly to the top of the basement stairs. She poked her head out of the doorway, listening again. There wasn't much of a chance that anyone would be home yet. Ned Wakefield, a busy lawyer in Sweet Valley, hardly ever got home before six-thirty. Alice Wakefield was usually tied up with her interior design business until then, too. But it never hurt to be sure.

When she knew the coast was clear, Jessica got out the yellow pages, then raced upstairs to her room. She put Prince Albert down on the bed, where he proceeded to roll around on the pile of blankets at its foot, snuffling and yipping as he tried to scratch his back.

"You keep quiet," Jessica muttered, thumbing quickly through the yellow pages. "You're the one who got me into this mess. Washing

70

machine, washing machine . . . ah, here's one."
Impatiently jabbing at the buttons on her phone,
Jessica dialed the number and tapped her foot
impatiently. "Come on, come on. Oh, hello!
Can you come to my house right now and re-
place a washing-machine hose? It's an emergency!"

With dying hope, Jessica listened to the repairman complain about how many calls he had
to make. "There's no way, lady. I could make it
by Friday, but not before then."

Prince Albert climbed into Jessica's lap as her
shoulders fell with disappointment. But she
never let a bad break get her down for long. No
one was going to do laundry for the next few
days anyway, she reasoned. So what was the
big problem? "OK," she said. "Let's make it
Friday afternoon. As long as you can be done
by five-thirty."

"Sure thing."

When Jessica had given him her name and
address, she hung up the phone, confident that
she had successfully handled the disaster. And
when Prince Albert offered to play tug-of-war
with a towel, Jessica joined in, laughing. In less
than three minutes, the whole incident was
forgotten.

Seven

Elizabeth brought a steaming bowl of green beans in from the kitchen and smiled at Jeffrey as she sat down. "Jessica's bringing the salad, Mom."

Even as she spoke, Jessica hurried in, setting the salad bowl down with a clatter. "There," she said breathlessly, sliding into her chair across from Elizabeth and Jeffrey.

"Well," Ned Wakefield began, serving up plates of chicken and potatoes. "I guess you must be all settled in by now, Jeffrey, huh?"

Jeffrey French passed a plate down to Elizabeth's mother and nodded. "The great thing about California is the sun. In Oregon, it was always either raining or just about to rain. I moved here so I wouldn't mildew."

With a girlish laugh, Mrs. Wakefield said, "Well, it looks as though you're pretty well dried out now." She sent Elizabeth an approv-

73

ing smile. "So how was your day, dear?" she continued, turning to her husband. "Did you get that injunction you were after?"

Mr. Wakefield nodded, his brow furrowed. With his dark hair, strong, athletic build, and gentle brown eyes, he was an attractive man to have for a father, Elizabeth always thought. "Judge Tyler's daughter is married to one of those developers," he said, taking a spoonful of beans. "And he didn't think that would make him too prejudicial to hear this—" He broke off, a look of surprise on his face. "What was that?"

Everyone exchanged a bewildered look. Elizabeth glanced nervously at Jessica, but her twin was concentrating on her food.

"What was what, Mr. Wakefield?" asked Jeffrey.

"I thought I heard something."

"I didn't hear anything, Ned. It was probably something outside," Mrs. Wakefield suggested.

Mr. Wakefield shrugged. "It sounded like it was from upstairs, but you're probably right. Anyway, when I found out about this I was really surprised—" He stopped again and put his fork down. "I could swear I heard something like, like some kind of howl."

Elizabeth's eyes riveted on Jessica. That time she'd heard it, too, and she knew exactly what kind of howl it was. Jessica looked up and met her twin's look of panic. "You know, I bet I left

74

my stereo on. I'll go turn it off." She pushed her chair back and dashed from the room.

Elizabeth met a questioning look from Jeffrey. He knew something was up, but she had decided not to tell him about Prince Albert just yet. Especially since it had been Jessica's idea, and Jeffrey had made his feelings clear on other occasions that he didn't like the way Jessica got Elizabeth to cover for her when she was in trouble. Elizabeth smiled weakly.

"Well, forget it. I don't want to talk about Tyler anymore." Mr. Wakefield leaned back in his chair and smiled affectionately at Elizabeth. "So, anything juicy for the 'Eyes and Ears' column this week?"

Suppressing a burst of nervous laughter, Elizabeth shook her head. Her gossip column for the school newspaper was always fun to discuss at dinner. Her family was sworn to secrecy about it. She had a sudden self-destructive impulse to say: "A certain pair of twins is keeping a dog in their house without telling their parents. When will the reckless duo get caught?" But she knew she couldn't.

"Not much," she said, trying to sound casual. She lowered her eyes as Jessica slipped back into the dining room.

"That's what it was," her twin said in a hurried voice. "I left my stereo on. There was some weird song on, with a lot of screaming and stuff. That's probably what you heard, Dad."

Shaking his head, Mr. Wakefield chuckled. "It sounded like a pair of wild dogs to me."

Unable to stop herself, Elizabeth started to giggle. She quickly clamped her hands over her mouth.

Her mother raised her eyebrows. "What's the joke, Liz? Something you want to share with us?"

Now Jessica started giggling, too.

"Not exactly, Mom," Elizabeth choked out.

For a brief, hysterical moment, both twins laughed uncontrollably, releasing the tension they'd been feeling.

"What has gotten into these two?" Mr. Wakefield asked, winking at Jeffrey.

Elizabeth recovered first. "Nothing. I don't know." She sighed and wiped a tear from the corner of one eye. She glanced at Jeffrey and grinned sheepishly.

"OK," Mrs. Wakefield said, giving up.

When dinner was almost over, Alice Wakefield said, "By the way, girls, I'm doing a load of dark clothes after dinner—I need my black cotton skirt for tomorrow, so if you've got anything, put it in the hamper."

"Sure, Mom." Elizabeth nodded. She looked across at Jessica and was stunned by the expression on her twin's face. Jessica was staring openmouthed at their mother, looking as if she had just been struck dumb.

"No!" she yelped suddenly, regaining her voice.

"I beg your pardon, Jess?"

Jessica pushed her chair back again and stood up. "I mean, no, Mom," she babbled feverishly. "I'll do the laundry for you. I want to. I know you've got lots of work tonight, so I'll just go do it right now, OK? Don't even get up! I'll do it right now. I'm finished eating. I'm stuffed." She paused for a moment, her hands clasped together and her blue-green eyes wide with panic. Then she dashed from the room.

Elizabeth resisted the urge to jump up and follow her sister. Something must be very wrong. Jessica was not in the habit of volunteering for laundry duty.

"I think Jess must have eaten some Mexican jumping beans, or something." Her father laughed, seemingly unalarmed by Jessica's bizarre behavior.

"Well, it's all right with me if she wants to do the laundry. You won't find me stopping her," Mrs. Wakefield said.

Elizabeth stood up, too. "I think I'll go see if she needs any help. Can you come with me?" she said, staring pointedly at Jeffrey.

His eyes widened with surprise. "Sure." He shrugged, giving her a strange look.

"Is there anyone here who doesn't want to do laundry?" Mr. Wakefield asked, an astonished smile on his face.

"Come on," Elizabeth said, pulling her boyfriend's arm. As they entered the kitchen, she whispered, "Don't look now, but it might be an emergency."

She yanked open the basement door, and the two hurried downstairs just in time to see Jessica on top of the washing machine, climbing out a high, small window with a laundry bag.

"Jessica!" Elizabeth cried. "What's going on? Where are you going?"

Her twin halted and stuck her head back in. "He ate the washing machine. I'm taking this next door to the Beckwiths'," she whispered hoarsely.

"What do you mean, he ate the washing machine? Oh, no." Elizabeth groaned and closed her eyes. "Jessica, we've got to tell Mom and Dad."

"No!" her sister shrieked. "If we tell them now, they'll never let us keep him. We've got to wait. Just until Friday. A repairman's coming then." She turned around and scrambled through the window.

"Oh, Jessica," Elizabeth moaned.

"Who ate the washing machine is what I want to know," Jeffrey said.

"Prince Albert. Our puppy," she whispered, looking nervously upward, almost expecting the ceiling to dissolve so her parents could see what was going on down there.

"Your *what*?"

"Shh!" Elizabeth took Jeffrey by the arm and shut the laundry room door. She pressed one hand over her eyes for a moment. "Don't ask me how I got into this—"

"Jessica," he supplied, a wry smile on his face. "Go on."

Elizabeth ignored the comment. "Anyhow, Jess brought home this puppy on Friday, and we—actually, she—thought it would be better to hide him so that we could prove having a puppy was no problem. If we had already had him with no accidents or emergencies . . ." Her voice trailed off as she glanced over at the washing machine. "I don't even want to look."

Jeffrey chuckled and put his arm around her, kissing her lightly on the nose. "I don't know how you put up with her, Elizabeth. I think I would have strangled her years ago."

"Now that's not fair," she said, defending her twin. "Jessica has a lot of very good qualities."

"Well, I guess I just haven't seen them yet," Jeffrey said sarcastically. "Maybe she only brings them out on holidays."

Elizabeth looked at him silently for a moment, trying to control her defensiveness. "She's my sister," she said finally, her eyes serious.

Jeffrey shook his head, suddenly apologetic. "I'm sorry, Liz. I know you love her. It just seems so incredible that identical twins could be so different."

"Well . . ." Elizabeth trailed off. That was

something she'd been wondering about all her life. She had been born four minutes earlier than Jessica, and it sometimes seemed that those four minutes made all the difference in the world. "Oh, well . . ." She sighed. "I've got her, and I'm keeping her. No matter what."

Just as Dana was changing the channel, the phone rang.

"I'll get it," Sally offered, starting to rise.

Dana sent Sally a strange look over her shoulder. "Don't bother. I'm up." She ran from the room to answer it.

The silence remained tangible in the room after Dana had left. Sally and Jeremy sat alone, staring wordlessly at the television screen until Dana came back.

"It's Mark Riley," Dana said in a strange voice. And as Jeremy stood up, she added, "But he says he wants to talk to Sally."

Jeremy froze and then turned slowly to look at Sally. He sat down again after a moment and focused his attention on a commercial, his fists clenched.

Biting her lip, Sally stood up, pausing uncertainly at the door. She looked back at Jeremy and then at Dana, her cheeks flushed with pleasure and confusion. She quickly left the room.

Before she was out of earshot, however, she heard Jeremy's outraged voice: "First she steals my room, then my best friend. I'm so *happy* our dear cousin is living with us."

Sally stopped, the blood draining from her face. For a moment she thought she might faint. So that was it, she thought. Jeremy was jealous. He didn't want to share Mark's friendship with her.

She perched unsteadily on a tall kitchen stool as she picked up the phone. "Hello?"

"Hi, Sally?" came Mark's voice over the line. "How're you doing?"

"Fine."

There was a pause before he continued. "I was wondering . . . would you like to see a movie or something tomorrow night? An early show," he added, his voice eager.

Sally took a deep breath. If she was ever going to win Jeremy over, she'd have to reject Mark. She couldn't give her cousin any excuse not to like her. "I don't think so," she said unsteadily. "I—I never go out on weeknights." She swallowed, blushing at the lame excuse.

"What?" Mark laughed, ignoring her rejection. "A big girl like you?" His voice softened and became more coaxing. "Are you sure? Maybe we could just go down to Casey's and get some ice cream. I'd—I'd like to see you."

Her heart pounding, Sally closed her eyes. All her life she'd dreamed of a nice boy, a boy like Mark, asking her out, wanting to be with her. And now she had to turn him away. "Really, Mark, I can't. I'm sorry."

"Well, maybe I'll stop by to see Jeremy," he said, laughing now. "After all, you can't stop me from coming over to see my best friend."

"No, I can't do that," Sally whispered.

"Well, I'm not giving up. As soon as the weekend rolls around, you won't have an excuse."

Sally stared at the refrigerator. She could almost see Mark say that, his serious face taking on the impish grin she had come to know during their brief meeting. "Well, I have to practice with The Droids. . . ." She trailed off, hating herself for what she was doing. Why didn't he get the message?

"Listen, I understand, all right? I'll see you in school tomorrow."

"OK. 'Bye." Believing she had just ruined her chances for a wonderful new friendship, Sally hung up the phone and walked dully back toward the den. But outside the door, she stopped. *I can't go in there*, she realized suddenly. *I can't go in there and have them both look at me, thinking I'm trying to take over.*

She turned and ran up to her room, fear gripping her. She couldn't make Jeremy like her. And Dana was starting to act funny every time she tried to do something for her. What was she doing wrong?

She paced back and forth. It was only a matter of time, she knew, before the Larsons saw how unhappy their son was with Sally there. They might be kind, but they wouldn't risk their own child's happiness for a stranger.

Shaking with bitter sobs, Sally flung herself onto her bed. If Mark didn't leave her alone, Jeremy would never forgive her, and the Larsons would make her leave. She'd have to leave Sweet Valley. Forever.

Eight

"Don't you have practice today, Dana?" Mrs. Larson paused, her paintbrush in midair. She was repainting the woodwork in the front hallway.

"Nope," Dana replied. "Guy had a dentist appointment, and Emily was absent from school. So we canceled." She turned to head up the stairs.

"Well, then, maybe you can find the time to pick up your room. I don't think the vacuum cleaner has had any action in there for quite a while. Now seems like a good time to do something about it."

With one foot on the bottom step, Dana stopped and stared straight ahead. She had every intention of using her free afternoon to go downtown to a late afternoon matinee. The Plaza Theater was running a series of Hepburn classics, and *Bringing Up Baby* was showing that day.

"Actually, Mom, I've got plans," Dana said carefully, her brow furrowed.

"I think they can wait. I'm serious about this."

Dana turned around, a stricken look on her face. "But, Mom! I was going to see a movie!"

"Dana, you spend plenty of time at the movies as it is. I want you to clean your room."

"What's the big deal? I'll do it later. I swear!"

Her mother continued painting, her mouth set in a determined line. "Of course, you could certainly do it later. That's not the point. I'd like to think you were responsible enough to keep your room clean without my having to nag you about it. You know, Sally doesn't seem to have any more free time than you do, but her room is immaculate. And she helps out all over the house. If she can do all that, I think you could manage to pick up your mess, Dana."

"Sally! It seems like all you and Dad can talk about these days is Sally and how wonderful she is."

Mrs. Larson stood up. "Dana, I am really surprised at you. Your father and I are doing what we can to make that poor girl feel welcome. And we have asked you and Jeremy repeatedly to do the same." She paused and crossed her arms.

Dana made no reply.

"Do you understand what I'm saying, young

lady? I want you to be a little more understanding about how we're treating her. And I think you could find it in yourself to be a bit more pleasant to her. Let's not discuss this any further, all right? Oh, and another thing . . ."

Dana's chest was heaving with suppressed anger and indignation. How could her mother pick on her like this? It had never happened before. Dana knew it wouldn't have if Sally weren't there. She waited silently for her mother to go on.

"I know Sally's too unassuming to ask to use my car, so I want you and your brother to encourage her to take it. I've already spoken to him about it."

Mrs. Larson gave a final brush stroke to the baseboard and replaced the lid on the paint can. She looked up at Dana, who was still standing on the bottom step, speechless.

"We keep the vacuum cleaner in the broom closet, in case you've forgotten."

Dana turned on her heel and ran up the stairs as her mother gathered up her painting materials. Rounding the corner of the hallway, she ran smack into her brother.

"Hey, watch it!" he cried, stepping backward. He looked at her closely. "Wow! Something got you! Let me guess. Mom just read you the riot act, too?"

Dana leaned back against the wall and crossed

her arms. "You know, this is really getting to be too much. I'm really kind of sick of it!"

"Join the club. I've been sick of it since before she got here."

"Can you believe how Mom is picking on me? I have to go clean my room now because Sally's is so immaculate. But she never cared about it before."

Jeremy was silent.

"You know what I don't understand, though," Dana continued, "is why Mom and Dad are acting so weird about it. It's not as if Sally was abused or anything."

Her brother snorted sarcastically. "I know what you mean. And now we've got to give up Mom's car! Tell her to take it! As if we don't have our own plans."

Her brother's remark reminded Dana of the movie she was going to miss, and that only made her angrier.

"God, I've really had it!" she declared.

"Yeah, right."

Dana was about to speak again when a footstep on the stairs made her whirl around guiltily.

"Hi, you guys," Sally said, coming around the corner. She looked from Dana's face to Jeremy's, and she frowned slightly. "What's up?"

Dana pushed herself away from the wall, her mouth twisted slightly. "We were just talking about how great it is that you have your driver's license. And we think you should take the car this afternoon to get used to it."

Sally flushed and shook her head. "It's no big deal. If you were planning on going somewhere, I don't care. Really. I don't need to go anywhere today."

"Oh, no!" Jeremy protested, digging his hands deep into his pockets. "We're both just hanging around with nothing to do. Go ahead and take the car. Stay out till dinnertime. Get to know your way around town." Jeremy's dark eyes were veiled; they told nothing about what he really meant.

Still looking uncertainly from one to the other, Sally nodded.

"Well, OK. If you really don't mind. I guess I could drive around a little bit, get used to the streets and—and everything." She halted abruptly and with a final look at her cousins, turned back down the stairs.

Dana exchanged a sour look with her brother and stalked into her room. "OK, we did it," she fumed, and slammed the door.

Downstairs, Sally asked her aunt hesitantly if it would be all right to take the car.

"Absolutely, dear. I'm glad you want to." Mrs. Larson gave Sally's shoulder a gentle squeeze as she pushed her out the door. "Have fun. And drive safely."

As she pulled out onto the street, Sally had half her mind on driving and the other half on her cousins. Something was wrong. She had interrupted something they hadn't wanted her to hear. She also had the unpleasant feeling that they had been talking about her. And, judging by the looks on their faces, they weren't being exactly complimentary, either.

But on the other hand, they had been so insistent about her taking the car. She didn't want to go anywhere—she had nowhere to go— but they seemed to want her to. She could never tell what she should do. Were they just being polite, or did they really not need the car? Sally shrugged, trying to shake off a feeling of despair. *I can't do anything right!* she worried. *How can I be such a jerk when it means risking this new life?*

Almost without realizing it, Sally had taken the route to school. It was really one of the few places she had been to since she arrived in Sweet Valley. She maneuvered up the driveway, past the sprawling front lawn, and drew to a stop in the parking lot.

For a moment, Sally just sat in the car, debating whether or not to get out. She couldn't think of anywhere else to go, and she couldn't face going back home just yet. With a sigh, she opened the door and got out, looking up at the glittering windows of Sweet Valley High.

Maybe she would just check out the *Oracle* office. She knew she didn't have time to write for it, but still . . . She wandered along the corridors until she found the office. Taking a deep breath, she opened the door and walked in. One of the Wakefield twins—was it Elizabeth? —looked up from her typewriter and smiled a welcome.

"Hi, Sally! Come on in."

Sally gestured apologetically to the door. "I just thought I'd stop by." She laughed, suddenly feeling at ease. "I'm sorry. Are you Elizabeth? I'm afraid I can't tell you and your sister apart yet."

"That's all right," the pretty blond said, coming forward. "I'm Elizabeth. And you're welcome to come in any time. I'm just finishing up my 'Eyes and Ears' column."

Elizabeth chuckled. "It's supposed to be a secret, but everyone knows that I'm the author. 'Eyes and Ears' is a gossip column—you know, who's dating whom, who might get the lead in the school play, that sort of stuff. Here, take a look," she offered, pulling the sheet from the typewriter.

Sally sat down and scanned with interest the neatly typed paragraphs, smiling at some of the sillier items. "This looks like fun. But how do you get all the information?"

Shrugging, Elizabeth explained, "Well, just keeping my 'eyes and ears' open is the best way." A mischievous smile crept over her face. "And it doesn't hurt to have a twin who's an incurable gossip. Jessica is several pairs of eyes and ears all by herself."

"Did you do a story about—" Sally paused, embarrassed to draw a blank on the names. "Oh, that's it—Maria and Michael? I hear about them all the time."

A guarded expression came over Elizabeth's face. "No."

"Oh, right, because it's supposed to be a secret."

"No, that's not really why I didn't," Elizabeth admitted. "I just think they're headed for trouble, you know?" She shook her head sadly. "It seems crazy to be so seriously involved with somebody you can't tell your parents about. I just have a bad feeling about it."

Sally's eyes widened with surprise. "But it seems so romantic!"

"I know." Elizabeth laughed. "My sister and her friends think it's the most exciting thing that ever happened at Sweet Valley. Anyway . . ." She leaned back against a table, dismissing Maria Santelli and Michael Harris with a shrug. "Are you interested in writing for *The Oracle*?"

"Oh . . ." Sighing wistfully, Sally shook her head. "I'd love to, but I really can't."

"Why not?"

"Well, I'm working with Dana's band, The Droids. Do you know them?"

Elizabeth grinned. "Sure, everyone at Sweet Valley is a fan."

"Well, I'm sort of their manager now, and I have to go to rehearsals, so I really don't have enough time. . . ." Sally trailed off, looking with yearning at the snug, cozy office, the bulletin board covered with notices and cartoons, the piles of dog-eared reference books. She sighed. "But I think I would rather do this. I love to write," she confessed.

Elizabeth's brow furrowed, and she sat down in a chair across from Sally. "I don't understand. If you really don't want to work with The Droids, why should you?"

Elizabeth looked so earnest, so sympathetic, Sally thought. More than anything else right now, she desperately needed someone to confide in, someone she could count on as a friend. And Elizabeth Wakefield seemed to fit the part perfectly.

Drawing a deep breath, Sally took the plunge. "It's Dana," she began, feeling like a traitor. "She really wanted me to, and, well, I hate to say no to her."

"Why? What do you think she'll do?" Elizabeth laughed. But she became serious when she saw how seriously Sally meant it. "Is it that important?"

"That important!" Sally opened her mouth and paused, searching for the right words. "If I don't make Dana and Jeremy—and my aunt and uncle—glad I'm here, well—" she broke off, suddenly embarrassed.

"What?" Elizabeth prodded gently, looking into her eyes.

Sally looked down at her hands. "I'm afraid they'll ask me to leave." She looked up, anguished. "I've had to leave so many homes. You don't understand."

There was silence in the room as Sally tried to control her emotions. With a shaky voice, she said, "You see, Dana didn't want me to tell anybody, but my mother abandoned me when I was a child," she said bitterly.

Before she realized it, she was telling Elizabeth all about the foster homes and the schools she'd had to leave. About the loss and pain she felt when her mother left her. It was such a relief to tell someone finally. But Sally's chin trembled dangerously as she finished her story. "Don't you see? If I don't do everything I can to be helpful and prove that I won't be a problem—" She stopped. It was impossible to continue.

Elizabeth reached over and touched Sally's arm. "I'm really sorry. I had no idea."

Because they were said with such sincerity, those simple words were an ocean of comfort to Sally. She managed a smile. "Thanks."

"But, Sally, I'm sure the Larsons love you and want you to stay with them just because you're you. You shouldn't have to go out of your way to be perfect."

Sally laughed bitterly. "Well, that's just the problem, because I'm *not* perfect. I mean, I can't seem to do anything right! Jeremy hates me, and I think Dana is starting to wish I was gone."

Elizabeth frowned. "Oh, I can't believe that. Maybe they're just having a tough time adjusting to you—you know, a new person in the family and all. It's not the easiest thing in the world, especially since you're so close together. Little things sometimes get blown out of proportion."

"You think so?" Sally looked uncertainly at Elizabeth.

"Sure, I think you should just give it time, and don't worry about it too much." Elizabeth cocked her head to one side, trying to coax a grin out of Sally. "And relax. Just give them a chance to get used to you."

Sally took some time to think over Elizabeth's advice. It made sense, but there was so much at stake! On the other hand, Sally wanted so much to believe this kind, sympathetic girl. She met Elizabeth's questioning gaze and smiled. "Thanks. I really feel a lot better talking about it. I just get so worried."

"I know what you mean," Elizabeth replied with a little chuckle. "Lots of times I get all worked up over something, until I talk to someone."

Sally nodded and stood up. "I think I'll be fine now. I mean it." It was true. She felt as if

95

she had finally made a real friend, someone she could talk to without worrying about making a good impression.

"Oh, by the way," she said, her brow wrinkled, "do you think you could not tell—well, I don't want anyone to know."

Elizabeth nodded, an understanding smile on her face. "I won't tell a soul, Sally. Honest."

"Thanks. I've got to go now. See you soon, I hope."

"Sure. See you tomorrow."

Sally left the office feeling relaxed and happy for the first time in days.

Nine

Sally tapped gently at Dana's door and held her breath until she heard Dana say it was all right to enter.

"Hi," Sally said, pushing the door open and poking her head inside. "Do you think you could give me some advice? I think you have a better head for this than I do."

Dana, who until then had worn a slightly guarded expression, now broke into her dynamic smile. "Sure. What is it?"

Feeling more confident with Dana smiling, Sally came in and sat on her cousin's bed, a brightly colored blouse in each hand. "Well, you know that skirt you helped me pick out last week, the one with the white stripes?"

"Yeah." Dana sat up, looking alert and interested.

"Well, which of these do you think would

look better with it?" Sally held out the shirts. She could tell that Dana was happy with her again.

She had learned quickly that Dana liked giving advice. Sally figured that Dana liked thinking she was guiding Sally's decisions. *So what?* Sally told herself. *If it makes her happy, that's all I care about.*

Dana squinted critically at the blouses. "I know," she said, springing from the bed in a burst of energy. She searched briskly through her own closet. "I think this would look best," she announced, pulling out a red shirt. "Why don't you try it on?"

With a sigh of relief, Sally nodded. "Thanks, I will. I'll be right back."

Hurrying to her room, Sally congratulated herself on scoring a point. Figuring out how to score was the trickiest job Sally had ever faced. She paused a moment, thinking that it didn't really make sense that there was so much pressure on her. She had hoped living with her uncle's family would be a lot more relaxed than living with strangers.

She stared blindly at the window, remembering the drive with her uncle the previous Friday night. The drive *home*, she thought silently, with a short, melancholy laugh. She shook her head; she didn't want to have unhappy thoughts anymore. She quickly donned the shirt and skirt. When she returned to Dana's room to model the new outfit, Sally saw her cousin's smile widen further.

"It looks great. I knew it would." Dana threw herself back onto her bed and smiled up at Sally.

Sally laughed. "If you don't make it as a singer, you could become a professional fashion consultant," she teased, delighted to be on a firmer footing with Dana at last.

"You'd better believe it! Say," Dana continued, rolling over on her side to get a better look at Sally. "Where'd you go when you took the car? You weren't out very long."

"Oh, back to school—"

"To school? Why?"

Laughing, Sally said, "I guess I just wanted to see what it's like when there aren't so many people around. You know, get a feel for it."

Dana rolled her eyes. "It's the same as during the day, just quieter."

Sally's eyes twinkled. "So I discovered." She paused, then said, "Oh, and I also ran into Elizabeth Wakefield at the newspaper office. We had a long talk."

"Oh?"

"Yeah. And she's so nice, Dana! She really is. And I think she likes me, too." Sally looked eagerly at her cousin. The Wakefield twins were two of the most popular girls at school. Sally had already learned that much. She hoped it would help boost Dana's opinion of her if she became friends with one of them. She hated to think of Elizabeth in terms of what her friendship could do for her, but she couldn't help it. It was so important to her.

Shrugging, Dana contemplated the ceiling. "Well, if you really want to be friends with Elizabeth, I can't stop you."

"What do you mean?" Sally asked, swallowing hard. Now what had she done?

"Well, I mean, you did commit yourself to us, the band, you know?" explained Dana, a hurt expression on her face. "And I guess you didn't realize how much time it's going to take up."

Sally stared at her cousin, not knowing what to say. What was Dana trying to tell her?

"But if you want to forget about The Droids and go after a busy social life, I'll understand," Dana continued. She stood up and wandered to the window.

One thing Sally had learned while moving from one foster home to another was how to read between the lines. If you weren't sensitive to what people were *really* thinking about you, you could get hurt. So there was no doubt in Sally's mind that for some reason, for some unknown reason, Dana didn't want her to pursue a friendship with Elizabeth Wakefield. And she was certain it wasn't just because of The Droids.

She nodded slowly and stood up. "Oh, I

see," she said thoughtfully, confused and troubled. She tried to shake herself out of it. "I never thought of it that way. Of course I'm committed to The Droids."

Dana's back was turned. She didn't answer.

"Well, I'll see you at dinner. I've got some homework to do."

"OK," Dana responded, her voice low. "See you later."

Closing the door softly behind her, Sally wandered down the hallway to her own room. Making friends in Sweet Valley was turning out to be a real disaster. She sat by the window, letting her thoughts roam.

It almost seemed, she mused, staring through the leaves of a nearby eucalyptus tree, that Dana didn't want her to like anybody but Dana, that Dana didn't want to share Sally's attention. And Jeremy sure didn't want to share his friends with her. Hot tears welled up in her eyes as she remembered how high her hopes had been. But she wouldn't mind, really, if they would only be nicer to her.

She sat bolt upright as that thought took shape, and her tears dried instantly. Why *weren't* they nicer to her, when she was breaking her neck to be agreeable and easy to get along with?

A rare spark of anger kindled in Sally's heart. Why did Dana want to keep her all to herself? Why should she have no other friends? Why should she do only the things Dana wanted her to do? It wasn't fair at all of Dana to act like that!

But as quickly as it had flared up, her resentment died down again. "Dana wouldn't do that," she whispered aloud, rubbing her aching forehead. She paced anxiously back and forth across the room.

Maybe she still wasn't trying hard enough, she reasoned, beginning to feel guilty for her angry thoughts. *Whatever it takes*, she told herself again, *whatever it takes to make them like me is what I'll do.*

She paused for a moment and drew a shaky breath. "I'm sorry, Elizabeth. I hope you can understand."

"Oh, Liz, you understand everything!" Enid Rollins's green eyes twinkled.

With a solemn face, Elizabeth replied, "Well, I do try. Now the question is," she continued, smiling at her best friend as she dished out vanilla ice cream at the kitchen counter, "what are you going to wear to this fancy lawn party you've jilted me for?"

"Very smart, Elizabeth. I thought that light green dress I got for that dance at the country club. Remember? The dress with the spaghetti straps."

Elizabeth nodded. She was delighted that Enid had canceled their shopping date for the next day because it meant her friend would be having a great time. The sudden invitation from a family friend was too good to turn down, Enid had said, her eyes full of optimism. There were bound to be dozens of good-looking guys there.

When Enid's former boyfriend, George Warren, had broken up with her, it had looked as though Enid would never get over it. The pain was gone by this time, but Elizabeth knew her friend still thought about him. Elizabeth had done everything she could for Enid, even going as far as trying to fix her up with Jeffrey French when he moved to Sweet Valley. Of course, that plan had backfired!

"That's a good idea," Elizabeth said, snapping out of her reverie. "It looks so beautiful with your eyes. And I can lend you that little embroidered purse of mine. It'll go really well."

Enid shook her head. "Eiizabeth, you're too much. I stand you up, and then you let me borrow the most expensive purse you own. But, thanks," she added. She suddenly sat up straighter in her chair. "I just heard something in the basement!"

"Relax, it's the repairman for the washing machine." Rolling her eyes, Elizabeth sat down across from her friend. "He's supposed to be out of here by five-thirty," she said, glancing at her watch. "And I'm sure Jessica is cracking a whip over him. It's almost five-thirty now."

"Don't you think it's pretty risky, hiding Prince Albert in the basement and Jessica's room?"

"Please!" Elizabeth commanded, holding up her hands in a gesture of refusal. "I have totally abdicated responsibility on this one. It's completely up to Jess."

There was a high-pitched bark from the basement, and the two girls heard Jessica's voice raised in a wail. "Fifty dollars?" Elizabeth and Enid exchanged wry smiles.

"Anyway," Elizabeth continued, forcing Jessica and her accompanying disasters out of her mind, "the only problem is, who am I going to go shopping with tomorrow?"

A look of mock dismay crossed Enid's face. "Oh, Liz, you're not really mad at me, are you? I'm really sorry."

"Don't be silly!" Elizabeth laughed. She thought for a moment. "You know, I think I'll ask Sally Larson to go with me tomorrow."

"Sally Larson? Oh, Dana's cousin, right?"

Elizabeth nodded, thoughtfully rubbing her chin. "Uh-huh, I think she really needs some friends."

"Elizabeth Wakefield to the rescue!" Enid teased, raising her hand into the air. "Fear not, all you sad, lonely people! Elizabeth will come to save you!"

Elizabeth stuck her tongue out. "Ha-ha. I really mean it, though. She stopped by the *Oracle* office this afternoon, and we had a long talk. I got the impression—" She paused, remembering her promise to keep Sally's story a secret. "I think she's been sort of lonely all her life," she finished with a rueful smile.

"Well, you're such a pushover, Elizabeth. I hope Sally realizes what a terrific person you are." Enid licked the last bit of ice cream from her spoon and smiled impishly at her friend. She suddenly became serious. "What about Dana? Aren't they hanging out together? I mean, it makes sense, doesn't it?"

With a shrug, Elizabeth turned away. She couldn't say anything more without betraying Sally's confidence. "Everyone needs more than one friend, Enid. I think I'll call her right now."

She picked up a local phone book and thumbed through it quickly. As she began to dial, she said to Enid, "Keep standing me up, Rollins, and I may desert you."

Enid chuckled.

The phone was answered quickly at the other end. "Hi, this is Elizabeth Wakefield, Mrs. Larson. Is Sally home?" She twisted the phone cord around her fingers while she waited. It seemed to be a long time before Sally came to the phone.

"Elizabeth? Uh, hi."

"Hi, Sally. I was wondering if you'd like to go shopping with me tomorrow? I need to get some new tennis shoes and some other things, and I thought you'd like to come along."

There was a short pause. Elizabeth's forehead creased as she wondered why Sally should take so long to make up her mind about such a simple thing.

"Well, I don't think I can, Elizabeth. I have to, uh—"

"It would only be a couple of hours," Elizabeth hastened to add. "And it doesn't make any difference to me when I go—morning, afternoon, whatever. We could go anytime you feel like it."

"Oh. It's just that . . ." Sally's voice trailed off for a moment. Elizabeth turned to Enid and frowned, shaking her head. Enid stood up and came closer.

"I mean, I'd really like to," Sally continued, her voice barely audible. "But I can't."

Frowning, Elizabeth shook her head. "Are you all right, Sally? You sound, I don't know— awfully tired."

"Yes, I'm OK. I'm sorry. But thanks for asking. 'Bye."

There was a click, and Elizabeth heard the dial tone. She pulled the receiver away and stared at it as if it could tell her why Sally had acted so strangely.

"What was the problem?" Enid asked, seeming to sense Elizabeth's concern.

She shrugged. "I don't know. She just said she couldn't." She shook herself and drew a deep breath. "Oh, well," she said with a bright

106

smile. "Looks like I have to go out by myself. You Benedict Arnold, you!"

"Don't start with me again, Liz!"

"Oh, now you're threatening me, huh? OK, I won't." Elizabeth laughed.

A few minutes later Enid left, and Elizabeth sat at the kitchen table thinking. She toyed with the saltshaker, her forehead creased.

From what Sally had told her that afternoon, she gathered there might have been some pressure on Sally not to accept Elizabeth's invitation. "But why?" Elizabeth said aloud. "How could she think that would make the Larsons like her more?"

Sighing, she rose from the table and straightened her skirt. If Sally wanted to tell her, she would, Elizabeth decided firmly. But until she did, it was none of her business. But thinking that didn't make her feel any better. With an uncomfortable feeling that she should have tried harder, Elizabeth left the kitchen and walked slowly up to her room.

Ten

"Mom's home," Jessica announced, hurrying through the bathroom that joined her room with Elizabeth's.

Her sister looked up, an unspoken question in her blue-green eyes.

"All taken care of," Jessica said, pausing to glance into the mirror. She smoothed back a stray lock of blond hair, and looking at her twin's reflection, added, "He's in my room."

"And the washing machine?"

Jessica smiled serenely. "Good as new. No one'll ever know the difference."

"Except me," Elizabeth said, closing her book with a snap. "Let's go."

"Liz, you worry too much. I'm telling you, dog ownership is making a new person out of me. I swear."

She received a skeptical look from her twin.

Pouting, Jessica opened the door and led the way downstairs. "You never give me any credit, Liz." She glanced at Elizabeth, looking for signs of softening.

"Well, if it isn't my favorite pair of twins!" Mr. Wakefield closed the front door behind him as his daughters reached the bottom step.

"Hi, Dad."

"Hi, Daddy."

He looked at them fondly and set his brief-case down. "So what isn't Liz giving you credit for this time, Jess?"

Jessica turned to Elizabeth with a grin. Why not give her a little scare? The prospect of such a dare set her eyes dancing with excitement. Turning back to her father, she explained. "This little kid, Albert, just moved into the neighborhood, and Liz doesn't think I'm responsible enough to take care of him."

Mr. Wakefield wore a puzzled look as he glanced from Jessica to Elizabeth. "Take care of him? Do you mean baby-sitting?"

Trying not to giggle, Jessica nodded. "Something like that."

"Well, I don't know, Liz. Jessica's done plenty of baby-sitting before. Why don't you think she should take care of Albert?"

Elizabeth hoped she didn't appear as flustered as she felt. "He's just sort of special, that's all," she said, darting an I'll-get-you-for-this look at Jessica.

110

"Who's special?" Alice Wakefield asked, walking in from the kitchen. "Hello, dear." She kissed her husband and looked at Elizabeth with an inquisitive smile.

Jessica knew her twin wanted to murder her at that moment, and she admitted to herself she'd been kind of mean. But it was so much fun!

"A little boy named Albert," Mr. Wakefield offered, kissing her on the cheek, "just moved in down the block."

"Oh, really? I didn't know anyone had moved in recently. How old is he?"

"He's—" Elizabeth began.

"Oh, pretty young," Jessica cut in, keeping Elizabeth from saying the wrong thing. "Just a baby, really. A mere pup, you might say." She glanced at Elizabeth's reddened face and burst into giggles.

Her parents looked confused. "That's nice, Jess," Alice Wakefield said with a tentative smile. "Who are his parents?"

"Jess, it's your turn to set the table, but I'll help you, OK?" Taking Jessica by the arm, Elizabeth steered her quickly toward the kitchen. "Jessica Wakefield, this is absolutely the worst," she muttered under her breath.

Once safely inside, Jessica laughed. "Oh, I'm sorry, Liz. I couldn't resist," she said, wiping a tear from her eye. She gave her twin her most

111

winning smile and giggled again when she finally got a smile in return.

"You're outrageous, Jess. I don't know how you can get away with it, but you always do."

"That's just the kind of person I am," Jessica said breezily, and she turned to go into the dining room with a stack of plates.

"I was thinking," she said a few minutes later, when the family was sitting down to eat. "Wouldn't it be fun to get a pet, like a dog? A cute, fuzzy little puppy?" She smiled hopefully at her parents, sure they would say yes immediately. "I could take care of him—it, I mean. I'd really like to."

Mrs. Wakefield put her fork down. "I don't know, Jess. You tried taking care of a dog once before, remember? And it was nothing short of a disaster."

"But—"

Ned Wakefield laughed. "Poor Mrs. Bramble. I don't think she ever recovered."

Sitting back, Jessica grumpily pushed some peas around on her plate. "That's not fair," she complained. "That was in sixth grade."

"And dogs haven't gotten any less dependent on good care since then," her father said, giving her a meaningful look.

"But, Dad! Why won't you even admit I might have changed? You said I could handle baby-sitting, and that's taking care of little kids! I think that takes more responsibility than taking care of animals!"

"It wouldn't have to be an expensive dog," Elizabeth put in, coming to Jessica's rescue. "I mean, we could get one free. Don't you think it could be kind of nice to have a pet?"

"What are you two doing, ganging up on us?" Mr. Wakefield laughed and shook his head.

"There's no such thing as a free puppy, sweetheart," Mrs. Wakefield added. She helped herself to salad and passed the bowl to Elizabeth. "There are vet's bills and licenses—not to mention dog food!"

Jessica glanced across the table to meet her twin's eyes. They held the same fear she knew her own did. What if their parents said no? They'd have to get rid of Prince Albert!

"But what if I prove I can take care of a puppy and keep it out of trouble and everything?" Jessica asked desperately, leaning forward on the edge of her chair.

Her parents exchanged looks of surprise. Mr. Wakefield said, "You're really serious about this, aren't you?"

Jessica's heart beat quickly as she nodded.

He shrugged, obviously unconvinced. "Well, I don't know. I don't see how you could prove that without actually getting a dog, and if it didn't work out, you'd have to take it back. I'll be honest with you, Jess. I can't help thinking this is just one of your whims."

Her throat tight, Jessica shook her head violently. "No! I mean—" She looked frantically at Elizabeth, unable to continue.

"I'd help take care of it, too," Elizabeth said, looking earnestly at their father.

He looked across the table at his wife. She raised her eyebrows and shrugged. He sighed. "Your mother and I will talk about it—"

"But, Dad," Jessica exclaimed.

"Now, wait a minute," he commanded, holding up his hand warningly. "I said your mother and I will discuss it. I'm not going to give you an answer right this minute. Getting a dog is a serious decision, and we are not going to make it at the dinner table. And that's enough said on the subject."

Jessica's shoulders drooped with despair. She had thought it would be so easy to convince her parents! But she couldn't give Prince Albert away. She just wouldn't. He was no whim! She loved him. Clenching her jaw tightly, Jessica decided to put it out of her mind for the time being. There was no point in getting hysterical about it. Something would turn up to make things right.

"Jess, did you hear me?"

She jumped. "What? I'm sorry."

"I said do you have a date tonight?" Mrs. Wakefield asked, handing her the milk pitcher.

"No. I'm staying in," she said, and with an elaborate yawn, she added, "I'm really exhausted from cheerleading practice. I'm just going to go to bed early."

That was a pretty unbelievable story, she knew. Cheerleading had never kept her in on a Friday night before. But she couldn't risk Prince Albert's howling or crying while her parents were home. He was quiet only when she was around to reassure him. She glanced guiltily at Elizabeth under her lashes.

But if anyone was skeptical, at least no one said anything. "Well, anyway," Mrs. Wakefield said, pushing her chair back, "I'll be out almost all day tomorrow. I'm taking a new client antique hunting, and I'll be leaving pretty early. So you girls are on your own."

"I'll be at the office, too," Mr. Wakefield put in, finishing off a pork chop. "This injunction is causing more trouble than it's worth, I'm afraid."

Jessica and Elizabeth glanced at each other. The coast would be clear on Saturday.

"Well," Jessica announced, trying to look as sincere and responsible as possible, "I'll be upstairs."

Sally paused at the top of the stairs, catching the murmur of voices below as the front door closed. Thinking she recognized the visitor's voice, she moved closer. For some reason, she held back, hating to eavesdrop but feeling that she couldn't go downstairs before she knew who it was.

"Is—is Sally home?"

It was Mark Riley. Sally's heart started pounding.

She wasn't surprised by Jeremy's answer. "I think she's busy," he said, his voice edged with irritation. "Let's hit a movie or something, OK?"

"Why don't we just hang out here and watch TV? There isn't anything I want to see."

There was a pause, during which Sally could hear her own shallow breathing. Mark was deliberately trying to stay, she realized. In a flash of intuition, she knew he had come just to see her. More than anything, she wanted to go downstairs to talk with him, be with someone who really liked her and didn't get angry every time she turned around. But her feet wouldn't move. She couldn't risk seeing the anger in her cousin's face.

The voices faded as the boys moved down the hallway to the kitchen. Sally closed her eyes, feeling utterly alone. With a heavy heart, she turned and walked silently back to her room.

Elizabeth was dreaming that she was lying on her back out in the rain. Her face was covered with moisture. As she awakened groggily, she realized dimly that someone was licking her face.

116

Her eyes flew open to see Prince Albert's fuzzy gold face looking down into hers. "Albert!" she cried, grabbing him in a hug that obviously delighted him. As soon as she spoke she looked anxiously around, as if expecting her parents to burst into her room, their accusing fingers pointing angrily at the dog.

"Relax, the coast is clear," came Jessica's voice. She stuck her head into Elizabeth's room, her mouth full of toothpaste. "Better get up. We're taking him for a marathon walk today."

Elizabeth chuckled. She threw back the covers and stepped out of bed. Prince Albert walked to the edge of the bed, tail wagging, and looked from the floor to Elizabeth. "Go ahead, you chicken. Jump!"

He lowered his head and then looked up, giving her an imploring look.

"That's a smart dog," Jessica mumbled through her toothbrush. "He's not jumping if there's anyone around to carry him."

With a giggle, Elizabeth cradled the puppy and placed him gently on the floor. "Boy, talk about getting the royal treatment. He won't be expecting a red carpet next, will he?" Elizabeth gazed fondly at Prince Albert, who was busily sticking his wet nose into every nook and cranny of her room. The only part of him visible at the moment was his behind with its wagging tail as he snuffled happily, investigating her closet.

The two girls quickly dressed, ate breakfast,

and then clipped a leash to Prince Albert's studded collar. "Ready for the great outdoors?" Jessica asked, opening the door.

He wagged his tail, and the twins laughed. "I think that means yes," said Elizabeth, following her sister outside. "Hey, Jess," she added, as they started down the sidewalk. "What if someone sees us with him?"

Jessica shrugged. "I usually don't spend much time outside with him. Besides, I figure by tonight Mom and Dad will have said yes, and no one will say anything before then."

Elizabeth stared at her sister in amazement. Jessica Wakefield could get herself into the most incredible situations, and she was in a new one almost every day. But no matter what happened, she always remained optimistic. She was absolutely unshakable. And Elizabeth loved her as only an identical twin could.

She shook her head. "Jessica, what would I do without you?"

"I honestly don't know, Liz. I—whoa!" Jessica halted in mid-stride as Prince Albert stopped in his tracks. "Well, come on, don't just sit there!"

But he seemed to have made up his mind not to budge, and he sat down, a stubborn gleam in his soft brown eyes.

"He's pretty strong," Jessica said anxiously, tugging as hard as she dared on the leash.

Elizabeth bent down and held her hand out to the puppy. "Come on, Albert, come on!"

The tip of his tail beat gently against the sidewalk, but he refused to move.

With a bewildered smile, Jessica said, "I don't get it. What's wrong with him?"

"I don't know. Try pulling again."

Jessica frowned. "I don't want to pull too hard. I don't want to choke him or anything."

Elizabeth shook her head. "Just pull gently."

Pulling gently had no effect. But suddenly, as Jessica tugged for the last time on the leash, the puppy put his head down and stretched out his neck. The collar slipped right over his head.

Paralyzed with shock, Elizabeth and Jessica stared speechlessly at the empty collar. Before they could collect themselves, Prince Albert turned tail and trotted across the street.

"Oh, my God, Liz!" Jessica shrieked, clutching her sister's arm.

"Come on! We've got to catch him!"

Spurred on by fear, Elizabeth and Jessica sprinted after the puppy, hardly stopping to check for traffic. They kept him in sight for at least five minutes as he bounded ahead of them as fast as his legs would carry him. They raced down the familiar sidewalks, calling out his name. But they quickly lost him in the maze of quiet streets.

Breathing heavily, they finally stopped at an intersection.

"What—what are we going to do?" Jessica panted, a stricken look on her face.

Elizabeth wiped her forehead with the back of her hand and shook her head. "Oh, Jess, I don't know!" Their eyes met. They couldn't bring themselves to admit it, but it looked as if they would never see their little puppy again.

They glanced down at the leash still in Jessica's hand, the empty collar still clipped to the end of it. It somehow made everything so final, so hopeless. Elizabeth thought of their adorable puppy, wandering lost and alone through the streets, and felt her throat tighten.

And then Jessica burst into tears.

Eleven

It was Monday morning, and Mrs. Larson turned from the stove with a frying pan in her hand. "Scrambled eggs?"

"Sure," said Dana.

"Yes, please," said Sally.

Jeremy grunted and stared intently at the back of the Cheerios box.

"Toast?"

"Yes, please."

A brooding silence ruled at the breakfast table for several minutes. Sally kept her eyes on her plate, slowly eating the eggs and toast her aunt had made. She took a sip of orange juice.

"Uhh-hmmm, kids," Mrs. Larson began suddenly, clearing her throat. She paused, as if unsure how to continue.

Sally looked at her. Out of the corner of her

eye she could see Dana and Jeremy looking at their mother, too.

Mrs. Larson smoothed her hair with a nervous gesture, and her gaze traveled rapidly over the others. "I'd like you all to come home right after school today. Your father, your uncle Hal," she added, smiling faintly at Sally, "has flown up to San Francisco for a meeting, and when he gets back he may have something important to tell us." Her serious eyes rested on Sally for a moment, then moved away.

The toast turned to sand in Sally's mouth, and she swallowed with difficulty. It was a meeting about her, obviously. And then the blood drained from her face as she thought, *He's arranging to have me sent to another home.*

The silence descended again like a cloud. Everyone at the table seemed to be deep in thought, speculating on what the news could be. There was no doubt in Sally's mind, and she had to force herself to finish her breakfast, force herself to keep her hands steady. She had failed again.

A chair scraped as Dana stood up. "Can we take the car then, Mom? We'll get home sooner."

"Yes, of course."

Dana looked quickly at Sally, who noticed the sharp glance. *She's thinking the same thing*, Sally thought. *She's probably relieved I'm going. She's tired of having me around.*

Feeling as though she were walking to a

prison, Sally followed her cousins out to the car and sat silently in the backseat, staring blankly out the window. A steady rain was falling, the first Sally had seen in Sweet Valley. *And the last,* she thought. *This is my last trip to Sweet Valley High.*

"Meet you here after school, right?" Jeremy was looking at her and Dana with a strained look on his face. Both girls nodded. "Right," he said, jerking the car door open with a frown.

Sally lagged along behind as the three walked across the parking lot. She watched Dana's long-legged figure striding ahead and saw her wave a greeting to a group of students. *I don't blame them,* Sally thought. *I wouldn't want a total stranger moving into my house, either.*

"Hi, Sally. What's up?"

She tried to focus her attention on the person in front of her. "Oh. Hi, Emily," she said, vaguely realizing that she wouldn't be going to any more Droids rehearsals.

Sally moved through her morning classes as if in a dream, feeling utterly numb. *Oh, who cares?* she asked herself, trying to blot out the terrible feeling of pain and loneliness that threatened to overwhelm her. *I've had to leave lots of homes. This one isn't any more important than any of those.*

She drew a deep breath and had to hold on to the door of her locker for a moment. But it *was* more important. It was so much more important than any of those other places. Those were just houses, places to stay. The Larsons and Sweet Valley were a home.

The desire to say goodbye to her new school finally drove her to the cafeteria. She certainly had no appetite. Pausing on the threshold, she surveyed without bitterness the students who took their homes and their lives for granted.

She meandered past noisy tables. Through the window she caught sight of Elizabeth Wakefield, who was sitting alone under a tree outside. *I should say something to her*, she realized with a pang of regret.

But as she approached, Sally felt she might be intruding. Elizabeth was staring moodily into space, a faraway expression of sadness in her eyes.

At that moment, however, Elizabeth looked up, and their eyes met. With a warm smile, Elizabeth beckoned Sally over.

"Aren't you eating?" she asked as Sally joined her under the tree.

Sally answered with a shrug, because she hardly felt capable of talking. It took an effort to say, "I guess I'm not very hungry. What about you?"

Elizabeth managed a faint smile and waved her hand in a self-effacing gesture. "Oh, I guess I'm not very hungry, either."

The two girls lapsed into silence. It seemed

that both wanted to share their problems, but neither could find a way to begin.

"I—I wanted to apologize again for not going shopping with you on Saturday," Sally began, twisting a piece of grass between her fingers. She glanced up quickly, her heart full. Nothing she had done had worked with Dana, so she could have accepted after all. At least she might have gotten one pleasant day. Now she had lost the chance. She would probably never see Elizabeth again.

"I—" Sally faltered, wishing she could bring herself to say goodbye, to unburden the crushing weight of her disappointment to Elizabeth. But she didn't feel she should.

Elizabeth's blue-green eyes grew even more serious "Sally, what is it?"

Tears came suddenly to Sally's eyes and blinded her momentarily. Angrily pushing them away, she stumbled to her feet. "It's just goodbye, Elizabeth," she choked out, and turned to run across the sprawling lawn.

Sally hid herself in her books during the rest of her classes and hardly even bothered to pay attention. She wouldn't be coming back, so what did it matter? When the last bell of the day sounded, she stared in disbelief at the clock. How could the time have passed so quickly?

Slowly dragging herself out to the parking lot, Sally tried to brace herself for the scene at home. But she had a feeling that nothing she could do would prepare her. It would break her heart, no matter how hard she tried to deaden the blow.

"Hi," Jeremy said gruffly as she walked up to the car.

She nodded, with a faint, painful smile. "Where's Dana?"

"We're picking her up by the auditorium," he replied, opening the driver's side door. His voice softened slightly for the first time since they had met. "Ready to go?"

"Yes." She slid into the front seat and buckled her seat belt. She felt light and weightless and had the crazy thought that she might float away if she were not anchored down.

Jeremy started the car and they swung around the campus to the auditorium, where Dana was waiting.

"I'm glad the rain stopped," Dana said in a breathless attempt at lightness as they pulled out of the driveway. "I hate the rain."

No one bothered to answer.

Dana slumped down in the backseat and tucked her knees up. Sally bit her lip. She knew Dana was trying to ease some of the tension, but it was really pointless. Still, it was nice of her to try.

Sally stared sightlessly at the scenery as they sped along, trying to envision moving away from Sweet Valley. Somehow her mind was blank when she tried to picture herself packing

126

again. It was as if in her heart she just refused to believe it could happen. But in her mind she knew it would.

As she steeled herself for the upcoming scene, she unconsciously registered two rough-looking hitchhikers along the side of the road. She also realized dimly that Jeremy had put on the turn signal and was slowing down.

"Don't pick those guys up," she said, suddenly snapping back from her inner pain.

"Why not?" Jeremy asked coldly, pulling off to the side.

Sally glanced out the rear window. The two guys were jogging toward them. One of them flicked his burning cigarette into the grass at the side of the road.

She leaned forward again, grasping Jeremy's arm. "I know that kind of guy—and they're a lot of trouble, believe me."

"Listen, I'm a big boy," Jeremy declared, with heavy sarcasm. "And if I want to pick them up, I will."

"But, Jeremy, I swear I know what I'm talking about."

"Jeremy, I don't think you should—" Dana put in. But even as she spoke, the two scruffy-looking guys opened the backseat doors and got in on either side of Dana.

"Hey, man, thanks a lot."

"Yeah," the shorter one said, giving Dana an appraising leer, "let's go."

Sally looked back at Dana and knew that her cousin was uncomfortable. One of the hitchhikers was tall and skinny and had greasy, unkempt blond hair pushed behind his ears. The other was shorter and dark and wore a faded denim jacket with the sleeves cut off. The two hitchhikers were sitting very close to Dana, closer than necessary, and they were trying to get her to talk to them.

"We're only going a couple of blocks," Dana said nervously. "We can drop you off at Madison."

The one with the dark hair draped his arm around her. "Hey, relax. We want to go farther than that. Right, Al?"

"Right," Al joined in, looking Dana up and down. "We got all day. Let's hit Kelly's."

Jeremy cleared his throat. "Uh, I'm just going to drop you off at the freeway entrance, OK? You can probably get a ride to Kelly's from there. We aren't going that way."

Al leaned forward and spoke through clenched teeth, his voice softly menacing. "Listen, kid. We're going to Kelly's. Me and Jim are thirsty."

Jeremy set his mouth in a taut line. "Now wait a minute! I was nice enough to pick you up—"

They laughed nastily. "Yeah, you're a nice boy," Jim sneered. "Now take us to Kelly's like a nice boy. Now." He tightened his arm around Dana, whose face had turned ashen.

"Let's just take them, Jer. Just drop them off, and we can leave." Dana's voice was strong, but there was an edge of desperation to it.

"Right, listen to the lady, Jer. Do it."

Jeremy opened his mouth to protest, but apparently he thought better of it. He clenched his jaw and stepped on the gas.

Next to him on the front seat, Sally's mind was working feverishly, trying to figure out a way to get her cousins out of this mess. She'd spent a lot of time on the streets and had run across this type of guy often. They were mostly hot air and rough talk—but some of them carried out their threats.

Getting a closer look at them was important, but she couldn't risk turning around. That would only call attention to her, and that was something she didn't want to do yet. If she was going to succeed, she had to take them by surprise. Better to remain slightly invisible. For the moment, Jim and Al were more interested in Dana than in anyone else in the car.

"So what's your name, babe?"

"It isn't babe!" Dana snapped, defiant but clearly nervous.

Jim laughed. "Well, you're a hot one, ain't you? I like 'em hot. Don't I, Al?"

"Yeah, me, too!"

Jeremy turned around, an angry scowl on his face. "Hey, look, you guys, I'm taking you to Kelly's. Just leave my sister alone!"

"Whoa. Look out, Jim. We're making him mad!"

At that moment, the seedy, wayside tavern came into view. The tires crunched on gravel, and the car rolled and bounced as Jeremy steered through the glass-strewn parking area. They rolled to a stop under a sagging neon sign.

"OK, get out, you guys." Jeremy's voice was tight.

"Sure, but there's a couple things we need first," Jim said, breathing heavily down Jeremy's neck. "Like your wallet."

Jeremy whipped around in his seat. "What the—"

"Or my friend here will think of something to take from your sister here," Jim continued, a sinister note creeping into his voice.

"Jeremy!"

He struggled to get his wallet out of his back pocket. "Now get out!" he said unevenly, throwing the billfold in the backseat.

Al picked it up and looked through it, an evil smile on his face as he counted the bills. "OK, man. But one more thing."

"What now?"

Jim leaned forward and laid his hand on Sally's shoulder, and Al draped his arm around Dana. Al grinned. "I think we'd like the girls to get out with us!"

Twelve

Dana was rigid with fear. Overeager Sweet Valley High boys were one thing. But these two! She had never had to handle anyone like this. She cringed, trying to shrink into herself, away from the two cigarette-smelling louts on either side of her.

"Come on," Al said, yanking her arm as he opened the car door. "Let's go."

Jim started to open his door, too.

"Wait!" The voice was Sally's, but it didn't sound like her voice at all. With that one word, she seemed to have turned into a different person—strong, capable, and commanding.

Sally turned around in the front seat and stared boldly at Al and Jim, running her eyes over them casually. She seemed to be appraising them, and finding them lacking.

The mood in the car suddenly became electric. Sally had taken control, and Al and Jim were visibly surprised by the turnabout.

"Yeah?" Al said, regaining some of his former bravado. "What are we waiting for?"

Sally shrugged, her eyes indifferent. "You're wasting your time with her," she said, nodding curtly at Dana. "Don't let her clothes fool you. She's a dead bore."

Dana's mouth dropped open. No one had ever called her a bore before!

"Come on," Sally continued in an apathetic voice as she opened her door. "Let's get out here. I know how to have a good time—even if no one else around here does."

Jim laughed. "All right!"

"Sally, don't—"

But her cousin cut her off. "Listen, Dana. I've had it with you and your perfect little world. Living with you guys was the biggest drag of my whole miserable life." Her eyes were cold as she looked into Dana's.

The two hitchhikers jumped out of the car and slammed the door. "Catch ya later, babe! Now," Jim continued, putting his arm around Sally and giving her a squeeze, "let's party!"

Dana sat back, staring at Sally. She was stunned. Could Sally be serious about this?

Her brother looked back at her uncertainly. She shook her head, dazed. She couldn't think straight.

"Go on. Get lost," Sally said harshly. She threw

Al a smile before looking back at Dana, who was too confused to figure out what Sally was doing.

"Tell your mom and dad I'll be late for the family meeting. I've got some partying to do."

As if suddenly awakened from a dream, Jeremy started the car and backed out, a grim look on his face.

"Jeremy! No! We can't leave her here!"

He looked at her sharply. "She said she wanted to stay. You heard her."

Dana looked out the back window at Kelly's. Sally was just disappearing through the door, flanked by Jim and Al. Even as Dana watched, Sally glanced back at the car, that same strange look on her face. Then she was gone, swallowed up by the dark, brooding structure.

"Besides, we're safely out of that mess," Jeremy continued defensively as they swerved back onto the highway. He drove quickly back toward town.

Safely out of it, echoed in Dana's mind. And then she knew. Now that her terror had eased off, she realized what that strange expression on Sally's face was. It was a mixture of fear, sadness, and maybe even a little relief, relief that Dana and Jeremy were out of harm's way. "Oh, God!" Dana shouted. "Don't you see? That was what she was trying to do!"

"What? What are you talking about?"

A feeling of deep shame washed over Dana,

but she quickly recognized that this was no time for regret. Bursting with nervous energy, Dana grasped her brother's arm. "We've got to go back there! We've got to get her out! She just did that to get us off the hook! Come on, Jeremy. Listen to me!"

She saw the realization dawn over her brother's face. Without a word, he pulled off the road. A car whisked past them, sending up a small cloud of dust. Brother and sister stared at each other mutely for a moment.

"We have to go back," Dana repeated, her heart pounding.

Jeremy clutched the steering wheel, his knuckles white. "God, what a first-class jerk I am, letting her take those guys on by herself," he said fiercely, the muscles in his jaw tightening with anger. "OK," he agreed, a deep flush coloring his face. "But we can't go back there alone. You know Kelly's."

Dana swallowed hard. Everyone knew about Kelly's, even if it wasn't firsthand knowledge. It had as bad a reputation as a bar could have. The police were constantly raiding it on drug busts and to break up fights. Without a doubt, the usual clientele would be the sort to back up Jim and Al, not Dana and Jeremy. They wouldn't have a prayer, going in there alone.

"What should we do?" Dana was dangerously close to tears.

She watched her brother scowl through the

windshield, deep in thought. Jeremy hit the steering wheel with his open palm. "Mark! He lives about half a mile from here. Why didn't I think of it before?" With that, he put the car into gear and shot back onto the road, tires squealing.

A tense silence invaded the car. Both Jeremy and Dana were anxiously counting the seconds before they could reach help. They pulled into the Rileys' driveway, jumped out of the car, and raced to the house.

Their furious knock brought Mark to the door in seconds, along with Ken Matthews, captain of the Sweet Valley High football team, and John Pfeifer, sports editor for *The Oracle*.

"Hi, you—" Mark began.

"You've got to come quickly!" Dana gasped, staring up into their startled faces. "We left Sally at Kelly's with two horrible guys, and we've got to save her!"

"Whoa. Whoa!" Mark bellowed, his face dark with alarm. "What are you talking about?" His eyes darted from Jeremy to Dana and back again. "Why did you leave her there?"

Jeremy caught his breath and quickly filled the three boys in, with interruptions and corrections from Dana.

"They wanted Sally and me to go in with them," Dana gasped, "and Sally—she—" Overwhelmed with guilt, she burst into tears.

Jeremy stood silently for a moment while Dana

135

collected herself. Then he shook his head. "All Sally's done since she moved in with us was be generous and try to help out and make us like her. And we've treated her like dirt!"

Dana's head snapped back, and her tears dried up. "You're right," she whispered, dragging the back of her hand over her tearstained cheeks. "But right now we've just got to help her!"

"All right! Let's do it! Come on," Mark cried, suddenly spurred to action. "Come on, John! Follow us!" he called, racing toward Jeremy's car. The others followed hard on his heels.

John jumped into his car with Ken Matthews and backed out of the drive, waiting for Mark, Dana, and Jeremy to get ahead of him. Soon the two cars were speeding toward Kelly's.

Anxiously biting her fingernails, Dana watched for the tavern to come into view. *I'll never be mean to Sally again*, she vowed silently. *How could I have been so stupid and selfish?* In a flash, Dana realized how hard her cousin had tried to make the Larsons accept her—and how desperately lonely she and Jeremy must have made Sally feel.

"Oh, God," she whispered, shaking her head in remorse. "I'm so sorry!"

One glance at her brother convinced her that the same thoughts were running through his mind. He was shaking his head, a fierce scowl on his features. "Please let her be all right," Dana prayed. "Don't let those guys hurt her."

Within minutes they were bumping over the rutted lane to Kelly's with John's car close behind. Soon they were out of the car and walking into Kelly's. It took them a moment to adjust to the gloom inside the bar. But Dana was soon able to make out Sally sitting at a booth, with Jim hemming her in and Al leaning across the table. Mark strode forward and clapped his hand on Jim's shoulder.

"What the—?" exclaimed Jim.

"Let her go!" Mark demanded.

Jim sat back, his eyes bleary from the whiskey he had been drinking. "Who are you, man? The girl's with us."

"Yeah," Al put in, reaching across the table to grab Sally's hand. "She likes us. Don't ya?"

With an expression of disgust, Sally wrenched her hand free and sat back, staring at Mark Riley, her eyes wide with relief.

He looked at her. "Do you want to go home, Sally?"

"Oh, Mark—"

"Hey, listen, man," Jim slurred, lurching to his feet. "She wanted to come with us. No one forced her to stay."

"Yeah, just like no one forced me to give you my money," Jeremy retorted, reaching around Jim for Sally's arm. "Come on."

Jim stumbled as Jeremy brushed past him, and caught himself heavily on the edge of the table. "So what's she to you, anyway?"

"My sister!"

All eyes turned to Dana, who suddenly found herself pushing forward to get to Sally.

"Yeah," Jeremy added, his eyes blazing.

As Dana reached the frightened girl, she saw an expression of utter amazement in Sally's eyes. Without thinking, Dana sat down and put her arms around Sally and felt her cousin's thin frame shaking with sobs. Jeremy sat down next to them, reaching for Sally's hand.

"Ah, jeez," Al sneered, his voice dripping with scorn. He rose unsteadily. "This is disgusting. Why don't you kids get out of here."

Suddenly, John Pfeifer and Ken Matthews were standing in front of him, looking very serious. Al backed up, reaching behind him for the edge of the booth. "OK, man. OK, stay cool. Jim," he snapped over his shoulder. "Let's get out of here."

Mark caught Al's arm. "How about giving back Jeremy's wallet?"

An ugly glint showed in Al's eyes, but he took another look at his opposition and dug into his pocket with his free hand, muttering obscenely. "Here," he said, tossing the wallet onto the table. "I hope you don't mind if we bought your sister a couple of drinks," he added with heavy sarcasm.

Jeremy stood up. "Just get the hell out of here."

The two looked as if they were going to

argue—or even start a fight. But they obviously thought better of it and slunk out the door.

Shaking her head, Sally sat up, pressing her fist to her trembling chin. "Oh, God, I was so scared. They wouldn't let me go."

"Listen," Dana said, her voice soft. "You didn't have to come in here, you know. We could have all stuck together."

Sally shook her head violently. "No. I had to do it. I thought I could handle it, and you'd be able to get away." She looked searchingly into Dana's eyes and then looked past her at Jeremy. "Did—did you really mean what you said before?"

Dana felt her own chin tremble dangerously, and she nodded quickly. "Yes. I really meant it. And we're so sorry, Sally. We'll make it up to you, starting the minute we get home."

"Yeah," Jeremy put in, nodding vehemently.

But suddenly Dana's heart started thudding in her chest. What if her parents wanted Sally to leave Sweet Valley?

Sally and Jeremy seemed to have the same thought, for an awkward silence closed in on them. Finally Sally shook her head with a weak smile. "Forget it. I hope you'll remember me, and think about me."

Dana squared her shoulders. "No. No, Sally. We're not going to let you go now." She looked

139

for confirmation from Jeremy. He nodded quickly. "We'll fight for you. We'll tell Mom and Dad we want you to stay and make them change their minds. It has to work!"

Thirteen

The drive home was like a dream. Sally sat in the back of the car, her hand resting in Mark's. From time to time, Dana looked back at her from the front seat with a glowing smile, and Jeremy kept up a constant flow of conversation about sports and school with Mark. She thought she had never been so happy in her life.

Mark gave her hand a squeeze, and she looked up at him. "You're terrific, Sally," he murmured, a look of unmistakable admiration in his dark eyes.

Her heart full, Sally smiled. "Thanks," she said, knowing she was blushing. She turned away, unable to meet the intensity Mark showed. It was more than she could comprehend.

As they turned into the Larsons' street, the uneasiness settled in again. What would they learn when they got home? Would it be too late?

"Dad's home," Jeremy observed unnecessarily. He had driven to the airport, and everyone was instantly aware of his car in the driveway. He stopped the car and looked back at Sally. "Don't worry. We can handle it."

"Yeah," added Mark, his clasp strong. "I'm coming in, too. I'll fight for you."

Sally drew a deep breath. "Thanks," she repeated faintly, opening the door. It was strange. The whole time they were on their way to Kelly's her nerves had been on edge. Her one thought until then had been to get Dana and Jeremy out of that mess. Once she was alone with Al and Jim, all she could think about was how to get away herself. There hadn't been any time to think about leaving Sweet Valley.

Now all the helpless despair she'd felt all day came washing back over her, in spite of the love she felt from her cousins and from Mark.

She stood looking at the house for a moment, dreading to go in. If she could just prolong this new happiness a little longer, she thought, maybe she'd be strong enough to face the Larsons' announcement. She knew she'd have to come crashing back down to harsh reality soon.

After a moment of melancholy reflection, she realized that the others were waiting for her and looking at her with sympathetic, expectant faces. She smiled bravely and started for the door.

Dana gave her a quick hug. "Let's go."

Sally nodded and stepped inside.

"Where on earth have you all been?" cried Mrs. Larson, hurrying into the front hallway from the kitchen. "We've been waiting for you for an hour! Oh, hello, Mark!"

"We have a good excuse, Mom," Dana began hastily. Mr. Larson joined them in the foyer. "We got into some trouble, but we're all OK, and—"

"Then in that case I think you should tell us about it later," her mother interrupted, looking at Mr. Larson.

He took off his glasses and folded them, a businesslike expression on his face. "Well, what are we all standing in the hall for? Let's go into the kitchen."

As a group they entered the kitchen and found seats. Sally kept her eyes on the floor, hoping she wouldn't embarrass herself and the family by crying. She twined her fingers together nervously.

"Well, now," Mr. Larson began, fiddling self-consciously with his tie. "I'll get right to the point. I was in San Francisco today to see the state child-welfare people."

"Dad!" Dana burst in. "We have to tell you—"

"Dana, please," Mrs. Larson exclaimed. "Let your father continue. Then you can speak."

Sally met Dana's anguished glance and quickly dropped her eyes to the floor again.

"Anyway, as I was saying, I went up with

Julian DeBrino—he's our family lawyer, Sally—to work out the details, and it's all arranged."

Jeremy stood up. "Dad, before you make anything definite I think you should know—"

His father silenced him with a look. "Jeremy, I know this is a decision that affects the whole family, but I'll thank you to remember that your mother and I are the heads of this family. The matter is settled, and that's that."

"Dad, no!" Dana wailed, covering her face with her hands.

Finally, Sally lifted her eyes to her uncle's face. "I understand, Uncle Hal. I'm sorry it didn't work out."

"Didn't work out?" Mrs. Larson's forehead wrinkled with a puzzled frown. She glanced uncertainly at her husband.

"Oh, Dad, please!" Dana cried, stepping forward to grab his hand. "We want Sally to stay! We really do!"

"Yeah, Dad. You've got to let her stay with us!"

Mr. and Mrs. Larson looked at each other, a dumbfounded expression on their faces.

"I don't think you quite understand," Mrs. Larson said, the beginnings of a smile on her lips. "Did you think we were going to ask Sally to leave?"

There was a heavy silence, until Mr. Larson chuckled. "Sally, we've just arranged to legally adopt you. If that's all right with you, that is," he added, looking earnestly into her eyes.

For a moment, the room was utterly still again, as if the earth had just stopped revolving. Then everything broke loose at once, with Dana and Jeremy laughing and hugging their father, and Mark loudly thanking the Larsons.

Sally sat in the center of this joyous tumult, her eyes brimming with tears. Mrs. Larson came to her and wrapped her arms around her, and Sally began to sob and laugh uncontrollably at the same time. Never in her most hopeful dreams had she dared to think that such a miracle could happen!

"Oh, Aunt Anne, Uncle Hal," she choked out, hardly knowing what to say. "I'm so—I'm so—"

"Sally, you're staying! You're our sister!" screamed Dana, swooping down on her mother and Sally with outstretched arms. "You're staying for good."

"Welcome home, Sally," Mr. Larson said softly. "Welcome home."

"That was John Pfeifer," Elizabeth announced as she hung up the phone. "He just told me the most incredible story about Sally Larson."

Jessica grunted inelegantly and continued peeling carrots into the sink.

"She was driving home with Dana and Jeremy, and they picked up some hitchhikers. They hijacked the car and made Jeremy take them to Kelly's.''

''Oh, no. Don't even mention that place to me!'' implored Jessica, rolling her eyes. She had been through a harrowing experience there herself and didn't like to be reminded of it. ''What happened?''

Elizabeth sat down, picked up a pencil, and began doodling on a paper napkin. ''Well, it seems that Sally somehow convinced the two guys to let Dana and Jeremy go, but she had to stay with them. So Dana and Jeremy went for help, and they all stormed into Kelly's to save Sally.'' She paused, staring into space with a smile of admiration. ''Maybe I should interview her for *The Oracle*. What a story! It's real human interest.''

''If you want human interest, you should interview me about how terrible it feels to lose a puppy!''

''Oh, Jess. We did everything we could. You know that!''

''I know,'' Jessica said, wiping away a tear. ''But I keep thinking we should have done something else—looked harder—I don't know!''

Elizabeth sighed. She knew it was no use lamenting about what they should have done. They had spent every spare moment scouring the neighborhood. Jeffrey had searched with Elizabeth and Jessica for several hours on foot, and even Lila had cruised the other end of town by car to look for the lost puppy. But even though Elizabeth knew they had done everything possible, it didn't make it any better. She was just as upset as Jessica was about Prince Albert's running away.

"Hi, girls!" came Mrs. Wakefield's voice from the front hall.

"Hi, Mom. We're in here," Elizabeth called, casting Jessica a warning glance.

Mrs. Wakefield put down her handbag and peeled off her tweed jacket. "Whew! I am bushed." She sat down across from Elizabeth, her usual warm smile lighting her face. "So, how were your days?"

Trying to force Prince Albert out of her mind, Elizabeth said, "Oh, you know, the usual."

"Jess?"

"The usual," Jessica muttered from the sink, her back still turned.

Mrs. Wakefield raised her eyebrows skeptically. "You two are a real barrel of laughs today. And just how many carrots do you intend to peel, Jessica?" she asked, getting up and crossing to the sink.

There was a huge pile of scraped carrots on the drainboard. "I think there will be plenty for dinner."

"Oh, OK." Jessica turned around, her lower lip protruding just slightly. She shrugged and met Elizabeth's gaze. "I'll be upstairs," she said, slouching out of the kitchen.

"I suppose I should ask," Mrs. Wakefield began with a sigh. She glanced at the door through which Jessica had just disappeared. "But this time I think I really don't want to know."

"Dad!" Jessica's piercing shriek came from the front hall.

Elizabeth and her mother stared at each other for a shocked moment, and then ran out to the foyer. There stood Ned Wakefield, a golden Labrador puppy in his arms. Unable to speak, Jessica stared at him.

Elizabeth gulped. "Dad! Where did you get him?"

With an indulgent chuckle, Mr. Wakefield pushed the dog's nose away from his face. "Now you cut that out! Well, your mom and I decided it would be all right to get a dog, so I stopped by the animal shelter on the way home, for a surprise!"

"It's a surprise, that's for sure." Jessica gulped. Her eyes were riveted on Prince Albert. There was no doubt that he was their puppy. He had the same soft gold fur and oversized paws. And he was looking from Elizabeth to Jessica with his joyful puppy grin.

"Oh, Ned, he's adorable," Mrs. Wakefield murmured, coming forward to pet him. "And that's my favorite breed, too. Don't you love him, girls?"

With a silent, wide-eyed nod, Jessica reached to take the puppy in her arms.

"Dad, I can't believe you decided we could have a dog," Elizabeth said.

"Well, you two did a number on us the other night. And your mother and I think it would be fun to have another member of the family."

The two girls looked at each other, and a huge grin spread over Jessica's face. Elizabeth laughed with relief and happiness. She stepped forward to kiss the golden puppy's forehead and winked at her twin.

"You know, I've got a great name for him," Jessica said, a mischievous gleam in her eyes.

Her father reached over to stroke Prince Albert's fur. "What's that, Jess?"

"Prince Albert," she announced, and laughed when the puppy responded with an ecstatic yip.

"Jessica! I swear he knew you were talking about him!" Mrs. Wakefield said with a delighted laugh. "And he just seems to adore you already!"

A firm rap at the door halted conversation for a moment, and when Mr. Wakefield opened it, Jeffrey French was standing there.

"Hi," he said, stepping inside with a smile.

Elizabeth could see the look of surprise on his face as he noticed the puppy in Jessica's arms. To keep him from saying anything, she quickly said, "Dad got us a puppy. Isn't it great!"

Jeffrey darted a quick look at her and then

grinned. "Hey, he's really cute, Mr. Wakefield," he said, his green eyes dancing. "Good choice."

Ned Wakefield chuckled. "Thanks, Jeff. I guess that makes it unanimous! Now, were you completely serious when you said you would take total responsibility for a dog?" he continued, looking intently at Jessica.

She nodded vehemently. "Absolutely, Dad. I'll take such good care of him. And he won't be any trouble at all. You won't even know he's in the house!"

At that Elizabeth burst into laughter. "Oh, Jessica! You're too much!"

Her twin grinned happily back at her. "I really am, aren't I?"

"Well, let's start dinner," Mrs. Wakefield announced, obviously sorry to get back to more down-to-earth matters. "Are you staying, Jeffrey?"

"Sure. Thanks, Mrs. Wakefield."

"Good. Come on, sweetheart. Let's find a bowl for Prince Albert."

As the two elder Wakefields went into the kitchen, Elizabeth shook her head in amazement. "I simply cannot believe Dad picked Prince Albert!" she whispered excitedly. "It's amazing."

"Oh, I know. You wonderful puppy!" Jessica breathed into his neck. "Welcome home. We missed you so much. I love—"

A furious knock cut her short, and the girls

looked at each other in surprise. With a shrug, Elizabeth flung open the door.

"Elizabeth! Jessica!" cried Cara Walker, bursting in on them. "You will never believe what I just heard— Hey, a puppy!"

"Never mind the puppy!" Jessica commanded eagerly. "What happened?"

Cara's dark eyes were huge with excitement, and she tossed back her long hair with an impatient hand. "I just saw Maria Santelli—" she broke off, suddenly becoming aware of Jeffrey leaning casually against the wall. She stared at him meaningfully for a moment.

"I think I'll go help out in the kitchen," he said, shrugging his shoulders and sending Elizabeth a smile. He pushed himself away from the wall and sauntered through the door. Elizabeth grinned at his back.

"What? What about Maria?" Jessica demanded when he was gone.

"She and Michael just got engaged!" Cara exclaimed.

Elizabeth was stunned. "What?"

"You're kidding!" Jessica shrieked, clutching Cara's arm. "Did she tell you that?"

Cara nodded vigorously. "But it's a huge secret, because they don't want their parents to know."

"But if they can't tell their parents," Elizabeth cut in, a worried frown on her face, "doesn't

151

that mean they probably shouldn't get married? Besides, they're still in high school."

"Oh, Liz, come on! Where's your sense of romance?" Jessica scolded, thrusting Prince Albert into her twin's arms. "So did he propose to her and everything?" she continued, avid for the whole story.

Cara shook her head. "I don't know. Maria could barely talk sense, she was so excited. And I think we should do something for her, have an engagement party or something."

"Did you tell Lila yet?"

"No, I came right here."

Jessica turned back to Elizabeth. "Liz, could you walk Prince Albert? Just this once, I promise. We've got to go upstairs and call Lila!"

Elizabeth nodded, hugging the squirming puppy and watching as Jessica dragged Cara upstairs by the arm. She heard the door slam as they entered Jessica's room.

Getting married? Elizabeth thought. That was crazy! How could Maria and Michael get married if they couldn't even admit to their parents that they were dating each other? Elizabeth shook her head, trying to see it as a wonderful, romantic adventure. But she couldn't. All she could see was deception and trouble. And somebody was bound to get hurt.

"I don't know, Albert," she whispered. "All I can say is I hope I'm wrong."

What lies ahead for Maria and Michael—happiness or heartache? Find out in Sweet Valley High #34, FORBIDDEN LOVE.

Special Offer
Buy a Bantam Book
for only 50¢.

Now you can order the exciting books you've been wanting to read straight from Bantam's latest catalog of hundreds of titles. *And* this special offer gives you the opportunity to purchase a Bantam book for only 50¢. Here's how:

By ordering any five books at the regular price per order, you can also choose any other single book listed (up to a $5.95 value) for only 50¢. Some restrictions do apply, so for further details send for Bantam's catalog of titles today.

Just send us your name and address and we'll send you Bantam Book's SHOP AT HOME CATALOG!